More Praise for **The Bear Bryant Funeral Train**

"In these complex, gorgeous stories, Brad Vice explores the darker corners of human hope and desire—the terror that love can bring us to, and the rage. Yet the stories are not dark. Rich and deeply intelligent, they illuminate the fullness of our lives, braiding regret with triumph, and grief with a searing, exultant glee. What a rare pleasure it is to read stories so brilliantly imagined, brought to the page with power and majestic grace."—Erin McGraw, author of *The Good Life*

"While they're perhaps an odd coupling, I'm sure both Mr. Bryant and Ms. O'Connor would be pleased to see their names on the cover of this debut collection. Brad Vice's smart, humane stories remind me why I love to read, remind us all what fiction can do when delivered with intelligence and compassion."—Tom Franklin, author of *Hell at the Breech*

The Bear Bryant Funeral Train

The Bear Bryant Funeral Train

STORIES BY BRAD VICE

The University of Georgia Press I Athens

Published by the University of Georgia Press

Athens, Georgia 30602

© 2005 by Brad Vice

All rights reserved

Printed and bound by Maple-Vail

The paper in this book meets the guidelines

for permanence and durability of the Committee

on Production Guidelines for Book Longevity

of the Council on Library Resources.

Printed in the United States of America

09 08 07 06 05 C 5 4 3 2 1

Library of Congress

Cataloging-in-Publication Data

Vice, Brad, 1956–

The Bear Bryant funeral train :

stories / by Brad Vice.

    p. cm. — (The Flannery O'Connor

Award for Short Fiction)

ISBN-13: 978-0-8203-2745-7 (alk. paper)

ISBN-10: 0-8203-2745-X (alk. paper)

1. Southern States—Social life and

customs—Fiction. I. Title. II. Series.

PS3622.I26B43 2005

813´.6—dc22   2005017313

This book is dedicated to my mother, who read to me

The Sugar-Plum Tree and Other Verses and *Goofy Minds the House*.

And to the memory of my father, the man who gave me the two things

I needed to write—love and discipline.

Lordy, lord, the crazy talks we have. If people could hear us they would carry us straight to Tuscaloosa.

Walker Percy, *The Moviegoer*

Contents

Acknowledgments

Fiction Publications

"Mule": Forthcoming in *Shenandoah*.

"Tuscaloosa Knights": *Five Points* 8, no. 2 (Spring 2004).

"The Bear Bryant Funeral Train": *The Carolina Quarterly* 55, no. 1 (Winter 2003).

"Report from Junction": *The Atlantic Monthly* 290, no. 1 (July–August 2002).

"Stalin": *Hayden's Ferry Review,* no. 23 (Fall/Winter 1998–99).

"Artifacts": *The Southern Review* 34, no. 4 (Fall 1998).

"Mojo Farmer": *The Georgia Review* 50, no. 1 (Spring 1996).

Anthology Publications

"Artifacts" was included in *Stories from the Blue Moon Café*, Vol. 3, MacAdam/Cage, 2004.

"Report from Junction" was included in *New Stories from the South, 2003,* Algonquin Books.

"Chickensnake" was included in *Best New American Voices 2003,* Harcourt Brace & Jovanovich.

"Mojo Farmer" was included in *New Stories from the South, 1997,* Algonquin Books.

The author would like to acknowledge his appreciation for those friends, teachers, and editors who helped make this book possible: Tim Parrish, Ted Solotaroff, Allen Wier, Kent Nelson, Josip Novakovich, Erin McGraw, Andrew Hudgins, Tom LeClair, Jim Schiff, John Drury, Don Bogen, Will Allison, Dick, Lois, and Gilda Rosenthal, Shannon Ravenel, James Olney, Michael Griffith, John Kulka, Joyce Carol Oates, C. Michael Curtis, Chelsea Rathburn, Lauren Mosko, Tiffany Curtis, David Walton, Molly Thompson, Gail Hochman, Meg Giles, Joanne Brownstein, and the entire faculty and staff of the Sewanee Writers' Conference past and present (especially Wyatt Prunty, Pinckney Benedict, Barry Hannah, Claire Messud, Alice McDerrmott, Margot Livesey, Cheri Peters, Phil Stephens, Greg Williamson, Juliana Gray, Danny Anderson, Leah Stewart, Leigh Ann Couch, Ronald Briggs, and Liz Van Hoose.)

    Thanks also to my family, both the Vice and Dyer clans, especially Sister Sabrina, Sister Yoma Kay, Sister Meta, Sister Mahaska, and Sister Heidi. Thanks also to pals old and new: Scott Hamner, Lance Hopenwasser, Sharon Sams, Ricky Groshong, Mike Everton, Jim Murphy, Brad Quinn, Rich Lyons and Richard Patteson. Thanks most of all to my father and mother, Leon and Dot Vice, for all they've done.

A very special thanks goes to Noel Polk, Nicole Moulinoux, and all the members of William Faulkner Foundation.

Shout out to Tom Franklin, Beth Ann Fennely, Brad Watson, Brock Clarke, Elwood Reid, and the rest of the SOBs and DOBs.

The Bear Bryant Funeral Train

Tuscaloosa Knights

And that's how it began. Three distant notes, high blasts on a bugle, then a drop of a minor third on a long wailing note. It sounded like an English foxhunt. We heard them coming a long time before we saw them.

"It's the Ku Kluxers," said Pinion, fanning himself with a ragged edition of the *Atlanta Constitution*. "They're having a parade tonight. Going to burn a cross out at River Road." He leaned back in his wicker plantation chair, holding his highball glass next to his ear at an angle, as if the whiskey were whispering to him.

It was September, and it seemed to me that I had spent the better part of the long hot summer here, drunk on Pinion's porch, waiting for my husband, John, to come back from Switzerland.

John was the newest physician at Bryce, Tuscaloosa's antebellum insane asylum, and Pinion had helped John tap into a hidden stash of state money to finish writing his book on suicide. It had been five years since the stock-market crash, when scores of respectable bankers and businessmen had jumped from Wall Street windows to their death, and there was a renewed interest in the treatment of self-destructive impulses. When John received his under-the-table funds, he decided he needed to visit a famous sanitarium in Zurich to do the last chapters properly. Of course, I wanted to go, having studied German at school, but he said the stipend was too small. I was pretty upset that my husband planned to abandon me here in this dinky town with nothing to do while he pranced across Europe.

So John asked Pinion to entertain me in his absence. John and Pinion were golfing partners at the Riverside Country Club, where the small-town Brahmin gathered to socialize. I used to go too and swim in the pool, but after a while the gossip about who was running around on whom got to be too much for me, so now I spent most of my days bored, reading magazines, smoking cigarettes in bed, and occasionally scribbling notes for a tawdry novel I was writing to amuse myself, something that would out-Scarlett *Gone with the Wind*. Somehow I felt lonelier with all those vapid, chattering women at the club than when I was really alone. Scribbling away in my bedroom, I looked forward to sunset when I knew I could visit Pinion on his porch and have a taste of something strong. Most weekends he was kind enough to break up the monotony and escort me to one of the University of Alabama football games, only there wasn't a home game tonight, so I guessed the Klan was providing the town's Saturday-night entertainment.

"Can anybody go?" I asked, leaning over the rail, trying to spot them. "Even a Yankee carpetbagger like me?" I took a long sip of my sugared bourbon and then pressed the cool glass to my throat. The evening sun had dipped under the horizon, and the clouds were verging from a deep Mercurochrome pink to black. The old gaslights, now filled with filament bulbs, came alive and lit up the street.

"Sure, Marla. Question is, why would anybody want to? Trust me, it's no Rose Bowl." A drop of sweat trickled out of Pinion's thick black hair and down his cheek. He set down his glass beside the serving tray the housekeeper, Odetta, had brought out to us. Then Pinion wiped his face with the back of his hand and dried his fingers on the leg of his tailored trousers.

I hadn't liked Pinion much when John had first introduced us. Pinion Knox was loud and blunt to the point of being vulgar. As the state legislator representing north Alabama, Pinion was in charge of institutional funding for Bryce and the university, and considering his manners I always secretly thought John only befriended him in order to advance his career. When I started my book, I even came to think of Pinion as the villain, a dark-haired, blue-eyed lawyer with a thirst for booze and women. But eventually I grew to like Pinion's loud laugh and I figured that his bluntness was really a sign of affection, maybe because his job obliged him to tell so many polite lies. Most days since John had left I would try to work on a chapter for a few hours after lunch. I'd write another seven or eight pages that would end with the fictional Pinion cheating at cards or deflowering a virgin. When I was done, I'd take a walk down Queen City Avenue and find the real Pinion drinking on his front porch.

"I'm surprised you're not out there marching with them. What, did your washerwoman forget to starch your sheets for you?" I turned and shook my empty highball glass, letting the ice chips jingle. Pinion reached for the crystal decanter standing on a silver serving tray. "I thought you told me your grandfather was a big muckety-muck, a grand titan or poobah or something. I thought you said he was with General Forrest in Tennessee when he started the whole thing up."

Pinion filled my glass. "I did. My granddaddy was boss of the real Klan in north Alabama when there was a reason for it. This club you got here now hasn't got any more to do with the *real* Klan than the Boy Scouts."

"I guess we'd better watch out," I said, pinching his knee. "Didn't I hear that last year they beat up some poor college boy for being alone with a girl in the backseat of a car?" As the guardians of white purity, the Klan not only hanged uppity Negroes, they terrorized anybody they deemed licentious—drunks, wife beaters, excited college boys fumbling under the petticoats of coeds. I'd even heard a story about a pair of careless adulterers who had been dragged out of bed naked and horsewhipped.

Pinion raised his fists in mock combat. "I'd kill a few of them sum'bitches before they even touched me with one of their ropes, by God. The sight of all that white trash under the sheets gets me hot enough to shit fire."

Seeing Pinion get all worked up tickled me. I covered my mouth with my hand. That was one of the things that was attractive about Pinion—he didn't sugar anything for me except my drinks. Pinion came from a long line of handsome politicians, all of them with a reputation for getting into scrapes. Like his congressman father, Pinion was a legendary brawler. Club gossip had it that when he was twenty, he suffered a yearlong suspension from the university for being the first student in two decades to break the rule against dueling. It was said that he put a rival SGA member in the hospital by shooting him in the knee with an antique pistol. Others said that when he was in Montgomery, Pinion frequently challenged other state senators to "step outside" if they voted against him, as if the rotunda were just another roadhouse tavern where men gathered to drink and smoke.

"Look at those bastards." Pinion stood up and pointed out over the holly hedge. Underneath the towering elms, three horsemen robed in white rode down the middle of Queen City Avenue. As they passed under a magnolia tree, lamplight glistened off its waxy leaves, surrounding the riders in a misty halo. One of the horsemen raised his hood and blasted the same four mighty notes on the bugle. Behind the troika stretched a long watery line of white figures marching side by side like an army of ghosts, their shapeless garments shimmering in the night.

Pinion stood up and took my hand. "Come along to the street," he said. "I want to show you something." Pinion had never touched me in a familiar way before, and I felt my face grow flush as he led me down the steps of the porch and onto the cobblestone walk. "Look." Pinion pointed at the Klansmen. "You see their shoes? Invisible empire, my ass. I know every one of them sum'bitches. Every one."

Moving at the hem of the white robes were pant legs and shoes, dozens and dozens of shoes. One pair of button-ups with terry-cloth tops, another heavy-laced pair splashed with mud, brown work boots, canvas sneakers, congress gaiters—even a green pair with knobby toes swung past. Pinion chortled. Only the thick holly hedge separated us from the street and the long line of marching shoes.

"What's so funny?"

"Only Bobby Pate would have bad taste enough to wear green shoes."

I laughed because he was laughing. "Who's Bobby Pate?"

"Just some fool that clerks down at the county courthouse. And there goes his boss"—Pinion raised his voice—"the honorable Judge Harris."

A hooded figure with shiny black loafers turned to stare at Pinion and me still holding hands. It made my spine tingle, but fear only fueled the giggles.

"That one over there will be teaching Sunday school in the morning."

That did it. I doubled over. I laughed so hard my bladder hurt. It was like laughing in class—you knew you weren't supposed to, and once you got started there was no hope of stopping.

A few more of the hooded figures turned our way, glaring at us through the hollow eyeholes of their masks. At the very edge of the long narrow row of shoes was a worn pair of saddle oxfords. Above them the sheets were twisted and out of whack. The left shoe stepped forward gingerly; the uncertain right shoe dragged behind in a dead limp. All of a sudden Pinion quit laughing. "I don't think I know that one. I wonder—"

"Wonder what?" I was still laughing, knees together, both hands on my sides. My bare toes curled in the lush zoysia.

Pinion shook his head and turned back up the walk toward the porch. "Nothing. Come on, let's go finish our drinks. And then if you still have a mind, we'll have a look at their damn cross."

In Pinion's bathroom, I tried to fix myself up a little in the mirror over the sink. I pulled a brush out of my purse and frowned as I raked it through my freshly bobbed hair. I'd had it cut last week because of the heat. On a lark, I asked the lady at the beauty parlor to dye it ink black, the way I used to keep it in my old Vassar days. The lady at the parlor didn't want to do it. "You have such a purty color brown as it is," she said. I told her it was my birth-day and that I was twenty-seven and needed a change. Finally I coaxed her into doing what I wanted but left angry because when I looked in the mirror I didn't find my old schoolgirl self, just an old-fashioned flapper. For a while I told myself I was ir-ritated at the beautician and the way she had made me work so hard to get what I was paying for. In New Haven or Pough-keepsie, if you had money to pay, people did what you asked—no hassles, quick, efficient. In Tuscaloosa everything was an or-deal. You couldn't go into the drugstore for a pack of cigarettes without getting into a twenty-minute conversation about the foot-ball team or the weather, or worse, getting a lecture—once, right before John left for his trip, an elderly lady minding the register simply refused to sell me a pack of Viceroys because she said it *wasn't righteous for women to smoke.* I was so angry, I went home and threw myself on the bed and had a conniption fit in front of John. He was sorting through his closet and he didn't even look at me as I screamed and cried, he just kept picking through his long thin suits, trying to decide which one would make the best impression on his colleagues in Zurich.

"You're being a baby about all this, Marla," John had said, pinching lint off the sleeve of a pinstriped jacket. "Be grateful I have work here. The people are not so bad. Besides, we could still be living with your father." My father had been one of John's pro-fessors at Yale. Even when we were courting, it had occurred to me that John's interest in me wasn't purely romantic, but in those days John had been gay and full of fun. We went to parties and danced around champagne fountains and shared bootleg gin with good-natured strangers. I stared at my own strange reflection in the bathroom mirror. When I'd given my hair thirty strokes, I put the brush back in my purse and gave myself a hard look. *What do you think you're doing, Marla?* I asked. *Just what in the hell do you think you are doing?*

When I returned to the porch, I found Pinion in his wicker chair reading the week-old newspaper he'd been using as a fan. "Look at this," he said. On the front page was an X ray, a black-and-white photograph of a fibula with a hairline fracture. The previous Saturday, our team, the Crimson Tide, had played Tennessee. During the game, word spread through the stadium that one of the Tide's injured players, a tight end from Arkansas, had asked to be cut out of his cast so he could take the field. The tight end scored two touchdowns and we bested Tennessee twenty-five to nothing. No one really believed the story about the kid having a broken leg at the time, but then on Sunday the *Constitution* did an entire article on him. The headline read: "Paul 'Bear' Bryant—First Place in Courage." Bryant was the "other end" opposite Don Hutson, Bama's star receiver. Hutson and the quarterback, Dixie Howell, "the human howitzer from Hartsford," made a powerful combination, and since I'd moved to Tuscaloosa, the duo had become the princes of the South. But right now, for a brief moment, all of Tuscaloosa's attention was focused on the superhuman Bryant. Pinion had spent the last five days unfolding the newspaper like a map and telling anyone who would listen, "If this Bryant kid heals, we're SEC champs for sure."

Pinion reached into the pocket of his trousers and produced a coin. "I'll bet you this silver dollar that our lame Klansmen there is this Bryant fellow. It's just the kind of stunt those muckrakers would pull, pandering to the fans. They're trying to run me out of office, you know."

I looked at the headline again: "Paul 'Bear' Bryant—First Place in Courage." "No way," I said. "I don't think he'd do it."

"You'd be surprised what a poor college student will do if you wave a little money or tail in his face." Pinion spoke as if he had had plenty of experience in such matters.

I reached over Pinion's lap and pilfered a cigarette from his pack of Picayunes lying next to the serving tray. "Well, only way to settle the bet is to go to the rally."

"I aim to." Pinion fished out his lighter. I bent down to the flame in his cupped hands. "All we have to do his wait for Puddin to get back with the car."

Puddin was Pinion's driver and had been his father's driver before him.

"Where is Puddin, anyway? You don't think he's in any kind of trouble, do you?"

"No. He's picking up groceries for Odetta. I sent him out over an hour ago. He can't be much longer. Maybe he'll come back with some mint for the bourbon."

Pinion prepared another glass for me. He swirled bourbon into the ice chips as I smoked. Picayunes are for people looking for a real smoke. Every drag felt like shards of glass settling into my lungs. By the time I had stubbed out the butt I was into a nice hazy buzz. Pinion handed me my glass, and then I decided I'd better have a seat on the porch swing a few feet from the wicker chairs.

I felt rather loopy by the time Puddin pulled up to the house in Pinion's black convertible. Puddin was breathing hard and shaking when he pulled up into the drive, and it took some doing to coax him out of the car.

"Did you see them, boss?" Puddin took his cap off and blotted sweat off his bald head with a blue bandana.

"Yeah, Pud. We saw them."

As Puddin told it, he had just finished loading up the car with groceries when the night riders passed. Puddin was the last customer before the clerk at Abernathy's locked up. The door had just shut behind him when he heard the bugle sound. Puddin had quickly raised the top on the car and hid under the steering wheel, praying that nobody would spy him through the windshield. He had been so frightened that he had stayed there, cramped and numb, long after the parade had passed.

"Poor fellow," I said, patting Puddin on the back. "That's terrible."

"I am too old for this aggravation," said Puddin, putting his cap back on. He stooped to rub his knees. Pinion took the two full sacks of food from the backseat and put them in Puddin's arms. "Go take the goodies into the kitchen for Odetta, Pud. Have her fix you a cup of coffee. You might ought to spend the night with us. I don't know if you want to go home in all this."

Puddin nodded and headed for the kitchen door at the side of the house. He turned around when Pinion began to put the top down. "Now where are y'all going?"

"Miss Marla here wants to see them burn that cross, Pud. You want to come too?"

Pinion winked at me and my bourbon giggles picked up again.

"No, thank you, sir," replied Puddin, biting down hard on the word *sir*. "Why do you want to take Miss Marla into such a spectacle as that? You know something sorry is bound to happen."

"Don't worry about me, Puddin, I'm a big girl," I said, waving good-bye to him.

Puddin shook his head. "Ain't nobody big enough to be out with those crazy fools." He turned his back on us and disappeared around the side of the house.

Pinion just smiled. When he was finished with the hood, he opened the passenger's-side door for me. After he got behind the wheel, he reached across me to open the glove box. His shoulder brushed against my chest, and I closed my eyes as he fiddled with the latch, trying not to blush again. When I opened them, Pinion was holding an ugly black revolver. He opened the chamber and quickly snapped it shut. Then he gave me a lewd grin. "Loaded," he said. "Just in case we smell some trouble on the road."

Within a few minutes, Pinion had turned off Queen City and we were speeding down University Boulevard. The stars appeared to be far away, maybe because on the horizon there was a dim orange light growing in the northern sky. We rode past the edge of the university's campus and turned left at Bryce, toward the river. As we passed the beautiful old asylum with its Doric columns and cupola, I noticed a dozen or so inmates standing on the expansive lawn. Was something wrong? I looked up at John's office window, which was, of course, dark. I imagined him up there smoking a cigar, writing in one of his green medical ledgers with the gold fountain pen I'd given him for Christmas. Below, most of the inmates were milling around barefoot in their bed clothes; a few of them stood stone still, looking up into the night sky as if expecting a lunar eclipse or a fireworks display. Two stringy-haired women clasped their hands around the bars of the tall iron fence that surrounded the yard. None of them waved at Pinion's car as they might have in the daytime. They didn't seem to notice our passing at all. It was unnerving, and for the millionth time I wondered why John had exiled us to this tiny country town inhabited solely by football fans and failed suicides. Before I knew it, my fingers had found their way again into Pinion's free hand.

He looked at me in a sort of pleasant mocking way and said,

"Hey, reach down on the floorboard and hand me the flask." The flask was wrapped in the crumpled folds of the *Constitution*. The paper had also printed Bryant's yearbook picture. Standing in his uniform, tall and handsome, he could easily pass for a matinee cowboy. We passed the flask back and forth, taking little sips as Pinion navigated the heavily wooded road.

Then out of nowhere, Pinion said, "You know the Yankees burned down the university during the Civil War, even the library?"

I shook my head. "No. I didn't know that."

"Yep, got all four of our books." He winked, and I grinned back. "A Polish mercenary named Croxton torched it. He thought Bryce was the president's mansion and ordered his men to burn it down, too. Luckily the soldiers discovered that it was an asylum before they carried out the order. Can you imagine what that would have been like, a hundred or so madmen on fire and screaming?"

I took a slug from the flask and handed it to him. "I think by the time you catch fire, you're mad. At that point, it doesn't matter where you've been living."

Pinion nodded. "True enough."

We continued down the road until we came to a large man-made clearing that gave a view of the Black Warrior River. On the shoal, scores of cars were parked bumper to grill in a semicircle. Women and children, some of them eating sandwiches, sat on the hoods of these cars. Men stood atop the running boards drinking soda pop. A few frat boys had brought dates. The boys had unfolded colored blankets down on the grassy sand and now held hands with their sweethearts through the handles of their picnic baskets.

A ring of a hundred or so spectators, all men, crowded around the Klansmen, who were standing in formation. Down by the banks, there was a huge weeping willow, its body arched across the water. A mound of red Alabama clay had been packed in front of the tree, and a tall lumber cross, more than twenty feet high, filled the night with orange flame. It shined over the murmuring crowd. The Klansmen nearest the cross must have suffered terribly from the heat; occasionally they held up their hands to shield their faces.

It was similar to the grand bonfires the university built on the quadrangle for its homecoming pep rallies. I remembered the way Dixie Howell had addressed the crowd the previous fall and how the fans had cheered at just the sight of him, waving their crimson-and-white shakers in the air. I glanced down at the newspaper again, and the handsome young Bryant looked back up at me.

Pinion let the car idle in the back of the makeshift parking lot for a while. When he finally killed the engine, he said, "Stay sharp, I want to be able to leave quick if we need to." I started to ask why, but then he took his gun out of the glove box and put it in the front pocket of his trousers. That alarmed me, but I kept my mouth shut. Pinion walked toward the crowd and I followed. A few yards from the weeping willow, there was a platform with a microphone. At the foot of the platform, four Klansmen held a banner that read, "Jack Jolly Klavern Tuscaloosa Knights of the KKK." The crowd began to applaud.

"They're getting ready for the speaker," said Pinion. "Here we go."

Sure enough, the lame Klansman limped up to the platform and stood before the microphone. I cursed. Pinion gave me a quick smirk.

But then came the booming voice, rich and powerful, spilling in waves over the crowd. I have to admit, for a moment I was spellbound: the hooded army, the ghostly speaker, the murmuring crowd, the burning cross silhouetted by the soft green branches of the bent willow, and the black sheen of the river reflecting firelight.

"Why?" shouted the speaker, "Why do you suffer? Because of the papist dictatorship in Rome. Because the Pope has his minions right here in these United States, and is, at this very minute, planning to overthrow our democratic government. Do you want to wake up one morning and find a dago priest in the White House? Do you know what he plans to do right here in Alabama? He's got it all worked out. He is going to hand Alabama over to a nigger cardinal!"

When he said that, something inside me broke, and then all I could think of was poor Puddin cramped and afraid under the steering wheel of Pinion's car. Suddenly I noticed that some of them had baseball bats and ax handles.

"Are the people of Alabama—in whom flows the purest Anglo-Saxon blood—going to stand for this humiliation? How will we face the challenge of the beast in Rome?"

Now I was beginning to suspect that I had actually won the bet, despite the orator's limp. The voice sounded older, like that of a middle-aged man, and surely that wasn't the vocabulary of a twenty-year-old footballer.

"By banding together in noble communion. We will fight to the last drop, together, for freedom from oppression. We must band together to fight the devilish plot of foreign potentates—"

I felt sick now. All that liquor and sugar had not settled well. "I don't believe this," I said, holding my stomach.

"What, about the Pope? Of course not. This is all just muckraking nonsense." Pinion scowled up at the speaker.

"That's not what I meant and you know it. Come on and get me away from these hayseeds."

"What did you expect, a Mardi Gras?" Pinion turned on me as if I had insulted him. "You're the one who wanted to come here and get educated. Wait a second." Pinion cupped his hand behind his ear. "He's gone to preaching on evolution. I bet this guy is hell on Darwin." Just as Pinion mentioned Darwin, the orator removed his mask and spread his arms as if trying to embrace the crowd. It wasn't Bryant, but a stout man with a shock of dark hair. Pinion forgot about me and glowered at the platform. "God almighty damn."

"You know him?"

"The bastard."

"What makes you say that?"

"No, I mean a real bastard. One of my uncle's little indiscretions. The country's thick with them. Dunwoody's the worst. He goes around claiming we're kin." Pinion squinted into the distance. "I thought I'd run him off years ago, but that's him. Wood's a real bad penny, I'm telling you. He's here to screw with me just like he did in school."

"In school?" I could see Pinion drifting away into a private world of vengeance. The expression on his face made him look as I imagined him in my novel, ruthless and cruel, and for a moment all that vicious country-club gossip seemed justified. Pinion put his hand in the pocket that held the gun. "That's him, isn't it? That's the boy you shot in school. You shot one of your own cousins and that's why he's a cripple."

Pinion grabbed my arm. "Who in the hell told you that?"

"I don't know. People talk." I jerked my arm free and thought about slapping him.

"He's no cousin of mine." Pinion lit up a Picayune and blew

smoke at me. Suddenly, I was more sad than angry, more afraid than sad. For the first time all night, I felt the old loneliness creeping in.

"Stamp it out!" roared Dunwoody. "Stamp out the worship of graven images just as we have stamped out the immorality and licentiousness in parked automobiles along our country roads and shameless nude sunbathing in this lovely spot right here."

"What kind of fool would want to do away with nude sunbathing?" Pinion asked, trying to start up with the mockery again.

"I want to go home now," I said.

"So go."

Slowly I stepped forward and put my arm around his waist, just to see what it would feel like. "Please, honey, take me home."

Pinion look at me from the corner of his eyes, annoyed.

"Please," I said again. That was all I could think to say.

"You know, Marla, you think you're pretty goddamn smart, but—"

"I'm sorry," I said. "You're right. I'm sorry. Please, take me home."

On the way home, wheeling down River Road, Pinion hit a man in a white gown. Like a startled deer, the gaunt little fellow had flung himself out of the woods and tried to cross the road in a mad dash.

"Look out!" I grabbed Pinion's arm, but it was too late. The man's body flipped up on the hood, and the next thing I knew, my head had bounced off the dashboard. Everything went black for a second, and when I opened my eyes I had a lap full of glass. The man on the hood of the car was bareheaded, and his glassy green eyes glared at me. His gown began to flood with jagged streaks of blood.

"Oh, my God, he's dead!" I shouted.

"Shit." Pinion opened the door and stepped out.

As he did this, the man came to and sat upright, jerking forward like a marionette.

"Are you all right?" Pinion moved to touch him. The man screamed as if Pinion were the one who had just come back from the dead. He jumped to his feet and screamed again and then ran toward Pinion as if to attack. Startled, Pinion balled up his fists but slipped before he could swing and fell onto the road. By the time I made it around the car, the screaming man had run past Pinion and fled into the woods, heading toward the river.

"Jesus, are you okay?" I helped him up.

"Yeah. How did he run away like that? How could he stand to move?"

"Shock," I said. "He could have broken every bone in his body and wouldn't know it if he were in shock." I didn't feel sick anymore. I was high on fear.

Pinion put his arm around my shoulders. "You're shaking," he said. "And you have a cut on your head." He reached for his handkerchief and pressed it against my head. I let my body relax as he held me.

"Is it bleeding?"

"Not much. Here, keep pressure on it." He took my right hand and gently moved it up to the cloth. Then Pinion walked around to the injured side of the car. "Goddamn it." Not only was the windshield shattered, so was one of headlights. Worst of all, the right front tire was blown. "I hate to say this, but it looks like we're going to have to hoof it back to town. You think you can?"

I nodded and removed the handkerchief. The blood on the cloth reminded me of the blood soaking through the little man's robe. "Who do you think we hit?"

"I didn't know him to look at him. And he was barefoot. What kind of sorry-ass Klansman can't scare up a pair of shoes? Probably nothing but ringworm under that sheet."

It took me a second to put it all together. "No shoes. Pinion, that man wasn't in the Klan. That was a patient at Bryce. He must have slipped over the gate and gotten loose."

"You're kidding."

"My God. What's going to happen when he hits the river?" I wondered out loud.

"Anybody's guess. If he keeps going that way, he's going to run into Dunwoody's group. They could get rough on him. Those boys are pretty keyed up. On a night like this, they're just looking for a reason to bust heads."

I imagined the little man, bloodied and bruised by pipes and baseball bats, the uncomprehending look of terror on his face as the Klansmen strung him into one of the tall oaks that lined the river. I closed my eyes and thought of the safest place I could imagine, my father's study, with his volumes of Thucydides and Herodotus lined up side by side on the shelves.

"Marla," Pinion put his arm around me and led me back to the car. He cleaned the glass off the seat and then sat me down, "Wait here, maybe I can fix the tire in the dark. We shouldn't walk home in all this."

"Would you sit with me a second?" I asked, drying my eyes. "I'm scared."

He looked hesitant but then walked around to the driver's side. I buried my face in his shoulder as soon as he sat down and cried hard. We stayed like that for a long time, Pinion's arms around me, patting my back and shushing me like a kid. But soon his other hand wandered down to my thigh. Pinion lifted my chin up in order to kiss me quiet. I started to open my mouth to kiss back but closed it again. Hadn't I planned this? Wasn't this what I wanted? But not here. "Wait," I said. "Not like this." But Pinion didn't wait, and what could I do—go limp, fight, scream? Do people ever get what they *really* want, anyway? The hand on my thigh rose up to my breast. I started to ask him, *Are you crazy, are you out of your goddamn mind?* But he kept my mouth filled with his sour-sweet tongue, rank with booze.

My hands started moving too, from his knee to his belt. With my fingers, I found the revolver in his pants. He stopped kissing me long enough to draw the gun and place it under the seat. As he did so, the unclaimed silver dollar I'd won fell out of his pocket and rolled under the clutch. I thought about the handsome young Bryant, about all his talent and courage and how I didn't seem to have much of either. Pinion's hand was under my dress now, and I knew that what he was about to do to me wouldn't take long, not as long as it would take to fix the tire in the dark afterward. I knew that tomorrow I would regret this whole night. I knew that I would be more alone when I woke in the morning than in all the time since John had left. Maybe after I nursed the hangover, I would work on my novel. Maybe the Polish mercenary would return from the dead to finish his arson and burn down the whole damned town.

As Pinion climbed on top of me, a stray shard of glass cut into my hip, but I didn't care. There was a cold fire in my belly, and it made me wonder what it would be like to burn all over, to be doused with lamp oil and set aflame and burn mad-crazy forever. Soon my thoughts were eroded by the powerful sounds of crickets, tree frogs, and whippoorwills. It was just something I couldn't get used to, how the forest around Tuscaloosa was so alive at night. I listened to the enigmatic music of the woods and watched the tiny stars glimmer through the open top of the convertible. The eerie orange light continued to pulse behind us in the distance. Pinion was on top of me now, pinning me to the seat, but I felt light, numb, and etherized. I couldn't help but sense that someone was spying on us from above, as if the stars I watched were watching back. Maybe the landscape itself had eyes, the stagnant marshes to the south, the mountains leering over us from the north, brooding over the town, bending all of us to strange purposes.

No sooner had I thought this than I saw another flash of white, a figure spying on us from the edge of the road. Had the man we hit returned? Surely not. I yelled for Pinion to stop, but he paid me no mind. I beat my fists into his back as he groaned.

"Someone's here," I screamed. I was sure that this time it was a Klansman with a horsewhip come to punish us. "They're here. They're here." I said. I slapped Pinion in the face, hysterical. He grabbed my wrists and pinned them above my head.

All about the car I heard footsteps. Not the orderly march of the parade, but a sound like wild-animal hooves. Pinion moaned, grunted, and rolled off of me. Just then another figure in white ran past, a woman. She had wild hair, and her breasts bounded up and down inside the white linen of her bed clothes. Two men followed, both of them screaming with glee like boys released early from school.

"Hell." Pinion had one knee in the floorboard, desperately trying to pull up his pants and buckle his belt.

I pulled my dress down over my waist and rose up on the seat. By then I could see them, maybe forty inmates running wildly, surrounding us on all sides, their eyes glowing in the lone headlight.

Running together, their bodies appeared to fuse into a single white monster, a pale hydra of madness. Some of the inmates moaned in otherworldly agony; some squealed and chattered like jungle birds. Pinion's hand lurched under the seat, searching for his gun, but by the time he found it they had all passed, the tails of their nightshirts disappearing into the dark. They were running toward the river, toward the orange light on the horizon, toward the burning cross, leaving us alone in the terrible silence.

Mojo Farmer

Mr. Tibby watches the dark field for the creatures with shiny eyes that come to feed off the garden. From his bedroom window he looks over the shoulder of a naked scarecrow to the feathers of young corn waiting to shoot into stalks. Rooted loosely in the ground are tendrils of purple hull peas squirming with potential. Moonlight glints off pie tins hanging from the stick arms of his scarecrow. They hang still. Their strings point straight into the earth as if gravity were magnified by heat.

Even in the middle of a dry spell, Tibby keeps his garden clean as a family plot, tidy as death itself. In the cool of every morning he rises to make his field immaculate. In the gleam of

sunrise he beheads violet morning glories and nut grass. He un-
earths coffee weed from under runners and shakes the precious
dirt out of the roots so it is not wasted on the intruder. Garden-
ing is ruthless work, making way for the struggle of young runners and Tommy Toe tomatoes.

Today Tibby rises especially early, since before work there is
ritual. He pulls a large trunk, painted red and laced with rotting
leather, from under the bed. He opens it and fingers the contents,
feeling his way through the inventory. A Bible held together only
by a rubber band holds four hundred and seventy-two dollars
among the pages of Acts.

Tibby, tall and lean, now kneels on the warped floor of his
small house. Item by item, he accounts for flowers pressed in
between the pages of a tattered hymnal, delicate petals of rose
and spider lily. A shortbread-cookie tin holds a sewing kit—fifty-
seven needles sunk into a fabric tomato pincushion and assorted
patches and thread. There are hunting trophies: squirrels' tails,
rabbits' feet, even a beaver pelt with the hot scent of mold. In a
cigar box lies his father's yellowing ivory straight razor. An enve-
lope holds his children's baby teeth. At the bottom of it all is a
wedding-ring quilt, a patchwork of vibrant colors filled with in-
terlocking circles. He unfolds it and removes a book of home recipes buried inside. Both were gifts from his mother. The quilt was
a wedding present. The book came much later.

Finding all in order, Tibby selects a jar of dirty marbles—a
collection he started after the last of his nine children had de-
parted for town—most of them found in the gravel road leading
up to his mailbox. He tosses it carefully onto the mattress. From
the cookie tin he selects a palm-sized sewing square and pins it

to the left breast of his T-shirt with one of the needles. A spool lands on the bed next. He seals the trunk with a lock of braided hair and shoves it back under the bed.

He hugs the bedpost and pulls himself onto the bed. His legs are numb as sausages. He has to spend a full ten minutes rubbing them, every nerve buzzing with the sting of blood. The fruit jar of marbles jiggles as he rises to his feet, still holding on to the post.

Across from the bed stands a pale green chifforobe with glass onion knobs. Tibby looks for himself in the mirror on its left door, but weak moonlight won't bring him into perspective. There is only the shimmy of his dark hands, never steady, in the corner of the pane. When the feeling returns to his legs, he opens the wardrobe. Inside are his wife's faded gingham dresses, hanging like unburied ghosts waiting in line for a chance to fly out. Tibby runs his hand down the hem of the one on the far left. The airy touch of cotton and the sweet decay of the rotting marigolds on the floor of the chifforobe preserve Dell in his mind.

It is only when Tibby is in Dell's closet that he remembers having been young. He has opened the door often to touch her clothes. He imagines how each dress would look if Dell were inside it, how it would cling to her thighs in the summer and fold about the knee. Her legs had been delicate and strong, like those of a deer, or even a slim young mule. And like a well-loved mule, she was happy in hard work. She was proud when her fingers brushed and braided her children's hair, and she was content in the smell of cornmeal and tea cakes that filled her kitchen. But she was also happy in the heat of the field, and never more so than when plucking horned green tobacco worms from growing tomato vines.

He sighs to think back further, to when Dell's dress made a mystery out of her legs. Tibby smiles to remember his fat mama laughing at him every time he came to supper, love-starved to the bone. With snuff under the blanket of her thick lower lip, she would chuckle like she had never wanted for anything. Mama had whispered in his ear, loud so his father could hear, "Don't worry, baby, Mama's got a recipe for every little thing." Charming Dell was the best thing that ever happened to him.

Tibby holds the dress up to his neck and smooths it over his round belly as if sizing it in the mirror. He squeezes the sag of his left breast as if trying to separate it from his thin torso. His chest aches.

An hour later Tibby has prepared and eaten a breakfast of eggs, buttered toast, sorghum, and coffee. The buckled linoleum floor has been swept, and he washes the dishes with Dell's frayed apron on. Feeling the kitchen is squared away, he spreads newspaper out on the kitchen table, then walks through the living room and out of the house. There is still no hint of the sun. The stars are just pinholes in a dark curtain.

The nest of cats living under the house is restless. Country cats are feral and tame all at once. More than twenty of them live under his house, and many are in heat. They walk as if on piano wire. They smell of blood and urine. Tibby keeps them all in petting condition. The ones with milk still in their teats are the most affectionate; the others walk coy circles around him as he discards scraps.

Tibby picks up a young tabby. Her eyes are wide and bright as a surprised possum's. He runs his finger over the cat's chin and down her back. He lifts her by the scruff of the neck, takes her into his arms. She lets him rest his palm on the top of her head, and Tibby firmly snaps her neck.

Careful not to break her ribs, he splits the cat open with his pocketknife and removes every organ but the heart. Tibby takes her back into the house and lays her on the newspaper-covered table. From the refrigerator he removes a Tupperware bowl filled with chilled flowers and stuffs her rib cage with dandelions, pink hibiscus, and the navels of black-eyed Susans. He spices the corpse with gingerroot, rubs fresh dill weed into her heart. With fishing line he stitches her from belly to throat. Then, carefully, he places her in the space between his T-shirt and overalls. Tibby holds her still next to his belly with his left hand; he cradles the fruit jar of marbles with his right. Dell's cotton dress is flung over his shoulder. A spade is waiting for him as he makes his way to the garden.

Tibby's heart is a treasure map inked with the secret graves of young cats and the fragile bones of birds. Even an occasional possum or woodchuck has come to rest warmly under the bed of his garden. He steps politely over every unmarked tomb. Only the formless scarecrow made of mildewed hay and gunnysacks keeps watch in the glint of dangling tins.

Tibby gently removes the stuffed cat from his belly and places her between the rows of young corn with his children's marbles. The earth is loose and dry, no more than sand and iron ore before a rain. He digs a hole. The bones of his hand tingle, the flesh on his fingers feels like gloves. His yellowing T-shirt and the red quilting patch over his left breast are soaked in sweat. When he closes his eyes, he feels the lids pulse like drum skins.

Tibby has a vision for this field. The tomatoes will crawl lively in their cages, producing huge roses of Big Boys and Whoppers well into August. Soon cabbages will thicken with elastic leaves, and greedy pea vines will lick every inch of available soil. Right here, the tongues of this young corn will shoot into green soldiers hiding gold and silver. The roots will twist into the spiced flesh of this cat, sucking the marrow from her ribs and holding her safe with a wooden fist.

The sun rises behind Tibby. Soon the cat has a thick mound of red dirt on top of her. Tibby knows that when the rain seeps into the earth, it will find this garden rich.

He approaches the scarecrow. Lumpy bats of hay make up its stomach and torso. Tibby makes an incision into the canvas bosom of the make-believe man. He punches his fist inside the hole and digs out a handful of damp hay, then fills the void with his children's marbles. He removes the red square from his T-shirt and uses it to patch up the wound. Then he robes the scarecrow in the dress, slitting open the back of the dress and sewing it together around the newly sexed scarecrow. She has an air of secrecy, is mute as the tubers he pushes into the earth in March. Her lips are stitched shut.

Tibby kneels down and folds his hands to pray. He asks for the clouds to gather and the winds to blow up for a long, slow rain. A good rain will wash away the telltale scent of the dead cat and make the pie tins titter. He hugs the scarecrow for support, finding it hard to rise. Slowly, Tibby's hands walk up the scarecrow's body. Although the sun has not yet cleared the horizon, Tibby feels it bearing down on him. Despite this, he is sure the rain clouds will come, so he will return to the house and lie down—just as soon as he gets back the feeling in his legs.

Still embracing the scarecrow, Tibby whispers to the side of her stuffed head. He speaks to her of children and grandchildren, of holidays, seasons, and the happenings of the year. He tells her his dream for the garden. He leaves her to watch over it, confident she will frighten off any mangy stray that would dare to dig up her sweet-smelling cat.

Stalin

All the old diseases are coming back to us. That's what my dad says. It's on CNN. Right now the 153 passengers of Southwest flight 003, Albuquerque to Oahu, are in danger. Not from rotten fuel lines or faulty landing gear, but from the air itself.

According to the news, a passenger off flight 003 was hospitalized in Oahu just a few hours ago and was diagnosed with pneumonic plague. Pneumonic plague is caused by the *Yersinia pestis* bacillus, the same bug that causes bubonic plague, both of which are still found in remote pockets of the New Mexico and Arizona deserts. Pneumonic plague resides in the lungs and can be transmitted through the air. It needs no blood carrier such as parasites to spread. The disease is particularly dangerous aboard airplanes because of the 757's ventilation system, which continually recirculates air through the cabin.

A diagram of the inside of the plane appears behind the Asian anchorwoman. Blue stick figures representing passengers are surrounded by red swirling arrows representing waves of contaminated air.

The big brother of the Black Plague loose—the implications are nothing short of medieval. I know. I know better than anyone. I am getting my Ph.D. in early English history. State school, no money to speak of, but the history is the same. Plague. A lot of good nursery rhymes came out of that disease. Ring around the rosie, a pocket full of posies, upstairs, downstairs—in 1348, a third of the English population fell down. They, too, thought the plague was in the air. They called the bad air "miasma." They wore garlic around their necks and kept the petals of sweet-smelling flowers in their pockets to protect them.

"Yesterday," my dad says, "they closed a school up your way. Five students and one of the teachers had TB. That's something I thought I'd never see again, not in my lifetime. But, God, the plague."

Dad is a retired history teacher himself. He used to be a principal but administration got to be too much for him. He just took early retirement this year. Leukemia. A school is no place to be weak or distracted. Schools are full of danger, and my dad understands the perils of education. That's why I'm home, just off a plane myself thirty hours ago. He's got his first round of chemo tomorrow.

For the first eight years of my life my dad's favorite book was Nikita Khrushchev's memoirs, *Khrushchev Remembers*. He read it more than twenty times. Dad was not big on books. He read every word of the newspaper and subscribed to *Progressive Farmer*, but *Khrushchev Remembers* was the only book that ever captured his imagination. Once, when I was in the first grade, Dad was reading it again, sitting forward in his easy chair. My mother was out. The TV was off, the house was completely quiet. I hated to disturb him, he looked so important reading his book, thick and black like a Bible. But I asked, "Daddy, why are you always reading that book?"

Dad put his arm around me as if he were going to whisper something in my ear, as if he were going to tell me a secret. Instead, he asked me, "Do you know who Nikita Khrushchev was?"

"Yes," I said, "a leader of Russia." I don't know where I had heard of him; TV, I guess.

"Yes," my dad said, "a leader of Russia. Well, when I was your age—no, older—Khrushchev said he was going to steal our children away from us. He said, 'Your children will sit on my knee.'"

I had forgotten that ever happened until a few months ago when my mother called to give me the news. My father, David Philby, was a good teacher, principal, and Little League baseball coach. He has a solid heart. He's a gardener; he watches out for weeds and grows fine watermelons. He is a deacon in his church, but a quiet Baptist. He loves his wife and the children he taught, and I think he especially liked his shortstops. But when I was seven years old and my father was principal of my school, I thought that was his cover—that he was a Russian mole, a secret agent just pretending. After all, he read strange books about the forces of history by men with names like Khrushchev and Lenin. My dad was born in 1939 and remembered Stalin perfectly—the Red Army overcoat, the strongman mustache. Stalin was one of the people from the past whom he spoke of with great clarity, as if he were an old uncle, or a grandfather I never knew.

Now I'm back home with my mother, in the kitchen, and my dad is channel surfing in the living room. He wants to find one of those nature shows, *Lions of the Serengeti* or *The Secret Life of Bats*. But on every channel it's either news or history. After the third circuit he gives up and turns to me again. "Do you ever think about Sissy Lynn?"

"No, not really."

"I've asked a couple of doctors about her mouth. They say it could have been gonorrhea." He touches his fingers to his lips. "It could have been gonorrhea in her mouth."

Sometimes evil little fantasies pop into my brain. Like one time at Christmas I walked into an antique shop to buy a present for my mom. She collects elegant platters, china, fine things for the table. She has a gift for arranging silverware. She is the kind of person who notices the heraldry of butter knives.

I was just about to pick up a cup from an ancient tea set, but instead I pictured myself pushing over its shelf. All these delicate cups and saucers shatter on the floor. And it doesn't end there because that shelf is standing next to another shelf holding a collection of Prague crystal, next to a shelf holding china dolls with real human hair. Before I know it all these shelves holding the world's most prized possessions go down like dominoes. The world lies wasted at my feet, and all because of one mean, irrational act. It is all because of me.

There is a silent movie inside my head that shows awful things. It shows me pushing blind children in front of cars. It shows me swerving to hit dogs on the side of the road. Once it showed me hitting a pregnant woman right in the stomach with a gloved fist. She keeps mouthing the word *why* over and over again.

"No reason," I say.

That one really upset me. For a long time after that I felt this black fish finning me in the stomach. It makes me wonder if I'm a bad person.

Every year at Walker Elementary, the school I thought my father owned, a nurse came to check our class for lice. She always brought a number-two pencil. It may have been a different nurse from year to year, I don't remember, but I do remember that up until the fourth grade I liked the nurse's visit very much. I see the nurse now as very slim, young. She is not really grown up, yet so much older than I ever thought I would be. Now she is just this airy, evanescent creature to me, an angel working the room with a bright yellow pencil. And for a moment that angel paid special attention to me.

I laid my head down on my desk and closed my eyes. Then one of her cool hands was on my neck, and the other stroked my hair with the pencil. It made me feel light. I knew if I were older I could ask her on a date, and she might say yes, because she knew, she knew better than anybody, that I washed behind my ears. She knew the soap my mother bought was lilac scented. If I were older I might kiss her.

In the fourth grade, everything changed. The nurse was not young. She was not pretty. She was a corpse. There was nothing but a mass of varicose veins in her hose. Her thin hair exposed her gray scalp. From the instant she entered the room I was aware of the sharp bones trying to work their way out of her skin. Her clavicle pointed out of the neck of her uniform like a finger.

When the teacher introduced her to the class, the nurse said,

"Hump." Her lips moved of their own volition. She looked like a bitter old horse, and she held her pencil like a sword. Her name was Nurse Ramsey.

She started her way around the room. The way she held the pencil was barbarous, all five white fingers wrapped around it. One after the other, the kids on my row dropped their faces into their arms: Scott Hamner, Sharon Sams, Lance Hopenwasser, Jim Murphy, Ricky Groshong, Emily Stinson, Sissy Lynn. It looked as if they were catching their own heads after she had lopped them off. And then the movie began. Inside my head, the unending reel: Nurse Ramsey holds me to the desk with one crowlike hand and rams the pencil inside my ear with the other, over and over.

With every replay I zoom in closer on the deep aperture of the ear. Soon I see down the waxy canal. I see the spidery cilia. I know the real name of the eardrum, the tympanic membrane. Tissue-thin, it shakes with every vibration. Then it is speared by the lead of the pencil. Deeper into the underlying cavity. The three small bones of the middle ear, I can see them hugging one another. I know their names too, the incus, the malleus, the stapes—destruction. Deeper into the inner ear—what had the textbook called it?—"the internal ear, the inner portion of the ear, consisting of a bony labyrinth that is composed of a vestibule, semicircular canals, and the cochlea."

By the time Nurse Ramsey got to my desk, I was deaf in my right ear. There was only a hollow din in it, as if I were under water, as if it were filled with blood.

But sometimes things turn out to be much worse than I ever could imagine.

"Lice." My mother said it as if the word itself were filthy. She glared at me as if I were possessed of an unclean spirit.

"Lice," she said, "is for trash. How did you get lice?" I was angry. I started to tell her exactly where I got lice, and exactly whose fault it was. But my father was standing over the both of us, and as I opened my mouth he gave me a look.

I had gotten this look before. After school Dad always wanted me to play catch. I was never a good baseball player. I was big and lumbering, with no coordination, no real talent for the game. My fingers never fit into the glove right, my pinky cramped and twisted. I couldn't make a pocket to save my life.

"All you need is a little practice," he said.

I never had the courage to say, "I don't want to practice. I don't want to play." Instead I slapped at the ball, dodged it. During practice one afternoon, Dad broke my nose with a fast pitch. He was tired of my playing with no heart. He said, "I am going to throw this ball as hard as I can, and no matter what, you are going to catch it." Within seconds my father's whole body was in motion, his right arm whirling through the air like a windmill. I never saw the ball.

I dropped to the grass, blood and snot everywhere. Dad brought me a wet cloth to wipe up with. He kept apologizing, "I'm sorry, I'm sorry, I'm sorry." I was crying. He was crying, but after a while he got tired of feeling guilty. He got tired of my being a baby. "That's enough, Will, suck it up." Dad's lips pressed in at the corners in disgust. His eyes rolled sidelong.

Suck it up, the look said again, there in the kitchen. So I just dug my heels into the linoleum and waited for the bomb. My mother was about to come down on me hard. She pinched my arm. "Who? Who was it?" I dared not betray my father at that moment. I would not give up Sissy Lynn.

I had sat next to Sissy Lynn for two months of that school year. She was new to Walker, and she was shy because she had no teeth. Everyone asked her why, but she never talked.

Some people are born with tails, some with webbed feet. A few are born with their hearts on the outside of their chests and live. Many people are born without wisdom teeth. Sissy Lynn didn't have any teeth at all.

My dad sat me beside her in the front row. I was strategically placed there to wall her off from the rest of the class. I never had the guts to ask about her teeth myself; my dad would've killed me, and what's more, I had better manners. But sometimes the questions got by me. Quiet whispers floated past, "Hey, what happened to your teeth?" Then she would start to cry. After a while, kids asked the questions just to see if they could make her cry.

She was a sad creature, an animal that wanted to be a little girl. Pale skin, freckles, waxy yellow hair. She was too skinny. She brought cornbread for lunch, and sometimes fruit. She mashed up the cornbread in her carton of milk, which she opened from both sides to make a bowl. She ate with a spoon. I knew only old people who did that, but they used buttermilk. She also used the spoon to hollow out apples, and she ate the shavings a teaspoon at a time. Sometimes she brought baby food: Creamed turkey. Creamed carrots. She cried most often at lunch.

I tried to talk to her, but she ignored me. That made me angry. Here I was, the only kid trying to be nice, and she wouldn't even look at me. That made me want to ask her, "Hey, who stole your teeth?" But I didn't. And I am glad I didn't, because if I had ever been cruel to her I don't think I could live with myself now.

She was not altogether unpretty as long as she remembered to keep her mouth shut, and that was perhaps the real reason she never spoke. I tried to pretend she was an ugly duckling. Maybe she would grow up to have pearly, straight teeth. But deep down I was disgusted by her. She was unwashed. She smelled like sour milk. And she was content to sit in sullen silence.

Every afternoon for two months I asked my father to move me away from her. He refused. Once he asked, "Don't you feel sorry for her? What if you were like her? What if you didn't have any teeth?"

"I'd kill myself," I said.

"Don't be dramatic," my dad said.

Then Sissy gave me lice. Even though I wouldn't tell my mom who had given it to me, I thought she was right. Lice was for trash.

"We need to shave his head, don't we?" Mom was irrational when it came to dirt, germs, uncleanliness. Like most mothers, she couldn't stand a mess.

"No." Dad rolled his eyes. "I brought this from the dispensary." He held up a carton of delousing shampoo. He put his hand on my shoulder and we left my mother sulking in the kitchen.

I was overwhelmed by a sucking resentment for my father. This was his fault. He made me sit by Sissy, just because I was his son. It was his mistake. But when we got into the bathroom he whispered, "I am sorry this had to happen." The apology cut into me and bled most of the bad feelings out. But I didn't say, "Okay, Dad, it's all right." If I had, maybe things would have been better between us for the rest of our lives. But I just shrugged.

Then my mother burst in without knocking. "Take off your clothes. I have to clean them. Everything. Your underwear, too." I blushed but did it. She snatched them up and left the room.

The shampoo was red and smelled like iodine. I knelt over

the sink and Dad lathered it into my head. My scalp tingled, my eyes burned. Inside the box there was a small comb. Dad raked translucent little corpses into the sink. Some were still clinging tightly to fallen hairs. I wanted to crush them with my fingers. I wanted to feel them pop. Instead, water took them down the drain. My scalp was on fire.

After Dad was sure my head was clean, he pointed at my genitals. "We better get down there too." He would not let me do it myself. He said he had to be sure. I closed my eyes and held my breath as he lathered my crotch. The burn was unbearable.

Then the phone rang. Mom usually answered the phone first, but after a couple of rings Dad went to get it. I got a towel and dried myself off. Then a shadow flickered across the wall through the venetian blinds over the commode. The shadows danced on the wall behind me like a grass skirt. I put my towel around my waist and stood on the seat of the toilet, hooked a finger in the blinds and pulled them apart.

My mother stood in our backyard beside the barbecue grill, a can of lighter fluid in her hand. She was burning my clothes, not just the ones I had worn that day, but all of the clothes I had worn to school that year. All the new shorts, all the knit shirts, the blue, blue, blue jeans, all burning in a pile on the ground. It looked like she was burning my whole class.

Then my father shouted something very strange. "The brute, the brute." From the next room, "The goddamn brute."

Brute, an odd word for my father to use. Two summers ago, when I got the news that my father was sick, I checked out two books from the library: the fifteenth edition of the *Merck Manual,* and a copy of *Khrushchev Remembers* in hardback, published by Little

Brown and Company, 1970. I know now that *brute* was not my father's word, but Khrushchev's.

I have learned a lot about Khrushchev, his rise to power, his words. In his speeches he often quoted Pushkin and Zola. Khrushchev was the son of a miner, and he himself was a pipe fitter for most of his youth, but an early party member. Dissatisfied with his lack of education, he applied to the Industrial Academy to learn metallurgy at the age of thirty-five. From there he became party president of the university, then a member of the Politburo. By 1935 he was in absolute control of the Moscow Regional and City Party Organization—he controlled all public works. Khrushchev was rebuilding the city for communism; he personally oversaw the construction of the Moscow Metro and made the trains run on time. But by 1936 his main job was security. It was his duty to make Moscow safe for Stalin. 1936 was a year of terrible purge. It was said by Khrushchev's superiors that he was a man who "was not afraid to get mud on his boots."

I know Khrushchev's role in the Inner Circle, the select group of sycophants with whom Stalin surrounded himself. I can list their names: Beria, Bulganin, Kaganovich, Malenkov, Mikoyan, Molotov, Voroshilov. None of them predicted Khrushchev would one day rule over them.

Most of all, I know how Khrushchev saw Stalin. Stalin was desperately afraid of being alone. Loneliness—that was Stalin's disease. He kept the Inner Circle close to him, not just because he didn't trust them, but because he needed them. Stalin and the Inner Circle worked together, drank together, ate together, vacationed together. They watched Charlie Chaplin movies together, they celebrated children's birthdays and wedding anniversaries together, they did everything but sleep together. Since Stalin suffered from insomnia, no one slept. There were just catnaps amid madness, and slowly, the loneliness crept into everyone, not just the Inner Circle, but Stalin's family, too. I know Stalin's family, his wife, his sons, his daughter. Most of all, I know what kind of father Stalin was.

In the chapter entitled "Svetlanka" there is a photograph of Stalin and his little girl. She has freckles and a devilish smile. She is holding what looks to be a bouquet of black flowers. Stalin has his arm around her. He is holding her very close.

Khrushchev begins: "Stalin's character was brutish, and his temper was harsh; but his brutishness didn't always imply malice toward people to whom he acted so rudely. His was an inborn brutishness." Khrushchev tells of Stalin's love to see those around him dance. Dancing amused him, in the army, the Politburo, the Inner Circle, and most of all his daughter, Svetlana. *Svetlanka* was her name in the diminutive, Stalin's term of affection for her. Stalin had invited the Inner Circle to celebrate the new year at his dacha in the last year of Stalin's life. My dad would have been thirteen.

There was Georgian folk music playing on the Victrola and everyone was drinking, dancing, having a good time. Mikoyan was the best dancer, and he did the *lezghinka*, a Caucasian folk dance. Bulganin had done some dancing in his time as well. "When I dance, I don't move my feet," says Khrushchev. "I dance like a cow on ice. . . . Stalin danced too. He shuffled around with his arms spread out. It was evident that Stalin had never danced before."

Just then Stalin spied his little girl. Svetlanka was not dancing. She was sitting down, exhausted. Stalin said, "'Well, go on, Svetlanka, dance! You're the hostess, so dance!'"

The girl declined. "'I have already danced, Papa, I'm tired.'" Her father grabbed her by the hair, dragged her to the dance floor, and shook her by the scalp until her legs began to move about. Her face was red. Embarrassed, she cried. "He loved her, but he used to express these feelings of love in a beastly way. His was the tenderness of a cat for a mouse. . . . He behaved brutishly not because he wanted to cause Svetlanka pain. No, his behavior toward her was really an expression of affection, but in a perverse, brutish form peculiar to him."

Stalin's wife committed suicide. His sons hated him. Svetlanka died a bitter alcoholic, exiled from the Soviet Union. Like a terrible toad, Stalin devoured his children.

Mr. Lynn came to pick up Sissy from my dad's office only a few minutes after my dad had taken me home to clean the lice from my hair. Mr. Lynn signed the register, put Sissy in a rusty Continental, and drove away. But Mr. Lynn never went home. Neither one of them was ever seen again. Sissy's mother went hysterical. She called our house again and again to beg for help—then to curse my father, to tell him it was his fault, to tell him he was going to hell. Losing Sissy almost killed my dad. He resigned as principal at the end of the year and got a job teaching American history at a junior high school, where the children were older. He quit administration. He said he wanted his summers off to garden.

Last night was the first time Dad and I have ever talked about Sissy Lynn. I am certain now she is dead. If history has taught me anything, it is that some are born dead, without hope. The stars were against her. She should never have been born at all. Dad doesn't think this way. He blames himself.

He thinks he could have done more. He thinks if he could have saved her, he could have saved the rest: the runaways, suicides, drownings, the one shot to death in a robbery, the one beaten to death after a football game, the raped cheerleader pushed out of a moving car, even the one who dropped dead of a heart attack in gym. That boy was slim, athletic, doomed. Most were car accidents. Last night, Dad told me, all in all, he had lost twenty-nine of them in exactly twenty-nine years. He knows their names, he can recite them in alphabetical order as if calling the roll.

Dad told me the social workers had been onto the Lynns, and had already threatened to take Sissy away. The lice would have been the last straw. He should have called the social workers before he called the Lynns, but he didn't. He wanted to take me home and wash my hair.

Brute. My dad used that word for Sissy's father. Now, when I imagine Mr. Lynn coming to steal his daughter, the old sepia-tone monster movie plays inside my head. I see Stalin, his overcoat full of pestilence and plague, full of all the diseases of the Old World; he waltzes into my father's office and signs the register. Stalin strokes Sissy's lousy yellow hair and kisses her dark, hollow mouth. His mustache smells of quicklime. He takes Sissy by the hand, dances her down the steps of Walker Elementary, and drives her away in his rusty Continental.

Afternoon, in the car, and now I'm driving. I turn on the air. Dad is beside me, Mom in the back seat. We are heading for the hospital. Nobody feels like talking, so I have the radio on.

Over three hundred bodies have been found in a mass grave in Bosnia. Most of the passengers of flight 003 have been sequestered and quarantined. Three of them boarded planes for Asia, two for Tokyo, one for Hong Kong. Seven are still unaccounted for.

Dad is looking out the car window. Offhandedly, he asks me

to swing by his school before we go to the hospital. Not Walker, but the junior high school where he has taught for the last seventeen years.

My mother says we will be late. I don't care; what could that matter? Through the rear view I take a glimpse at her, still handsome and well kept. She has a smooth, brave face, not a hair out of place. What is important now is warding off fear. Decorum, punctuality, order—these are things that ward off fear. For her, arriving on time means that time isn't running out.

When we pass the school, kids are waiting in crooked lines for their buses to arrive. Others are ducking into cars. Who is watching them? Dad once told me, "When I was a kid I was only afraid of two things—the Russians and polio. We thought communism was infectious, because we actually believed in the domino theory, and that scared us. But polio was much worse. Nobody knew anything about it. My parents wouldn't let me go swimming. They thought you could catch it in the water. They just. . . ." He shook his head. "They just didn't know."

Caution singles out my father from most other men I have met in my life. When I was in the first grade he used to watch me so carefully it scared me. That's why I thought he was a spy. At noon, he stalked the perimeter of the lunchroom counting heads, compiling information. In the afternoon, when the last yellow buses had pulled out, my dad stayed behind looking for the left book, the lost backpack, the dead drop containing typhoid, diptheria, polio.

Dad is looking far out the window. In the first line there is a tiny blond girl who says, "Hey, there goes Mr. Philby."

Dad waves. He looks as if he may cry. At first, this does not touch me, but makes me angry. A bad movie begins, the one where I get back at him for being my father. The one where he is crying like a child, and I say, "Suck it up, Dad." But I start thinking about the *Merck Manual*. I never looked up leukemia. What happens when your own blood turns against you? I don't know. I don't want to know.

In the rearview mirror I see a row of sulphur-yellow buses pull in behind us, stop, and open their doors. Still waving good-bye, the blond girl leads the crooked line of children into the bus's interior and disappears.

Artifacts

It seems Margaret has been in the kitchen since the beginning of time. Since sunlight she's been cooking—kneading dough for bread, chopping, slicing, measuring out her day on the big oak counter next to the stove. Every few minutes she stops and scribbles ideas on a yellow pad with a grease pencil. The manuscript for Margaret's second book, *Voyages of the Dinner Table,* is due in Birmingham in two days. The book is being pitched as a "culinary spell book," a "gastronomic grimoire" even, and she is trying to make sure the recipes are truly magic before they reach Ann H. Hardy, her editor.

Margaret can prepare nine recipes at once, but it makes her feel more like a juggler than a cook: moving from notebook to cutting board, then from board to skillet to oven and back to the cutting board again. By the end of the month the book will have traveled from the desk of Ann H. Hardy into the test kitchens of Southern Progress Publications, where eight highly trained home economists will work in secret to weed out any dishes they find overcomplicated, irreproducible, or "esoteric." That was the word Ann H. Hardy used to describe five entrees that didn't make the final cut for *The Ashevillian,* Margaret's first book.

But Margaret isn't worried about tests now; she's put the corporate kitchens out of her mind. She is summoning all her powers to prepare one of the most esoteric dishes in the new book.

She is going to make Chocolate Duck.

She begins by pouring two cups of red wine and two cups of beef stock into a saucepan, then she waits for the mix to simmer. While she waits, she pours herself a glass of wine. Wine is something of a hobby for her husband, Dan. He had the carpenter make a rack that stretches all the way around the kitchen, just shy of the ceiling, atop Margaret's cabinets; he got the idea from a magazine. The rack accommodates more than two hundred bottles of wine, cheap merlots and cab sauvs from South America and the Sonoma Valley mostly; a couple of the Italians are worth something. Sometimes she wonders if keeping them here is a good idea: they're too high, and exposed to heat. Dan likes the look of them, though. He says they look like soldiers, all lined up like that.

The dark smell of warm beef and wine makes Margaret think of blood. It reminds her of the Victorian ladies in their corsets and petticoats who used to stroll to the slaughterhouse every afternoon for a fresh glass of it. In the nineteenth century, doctors told housewives that drinking blood staved off consumption. The glass of wine stays on the counter.

Margaret would not have made a very good Victorian. There is something too equestrian about the way she moves through the kitchen, the way she holds her stainless-steel utensils in the air, the tilt of her wrist when she swirls her copper pots over the open flame of the stove. Margaret doesn't bake bread so much as command it to rise and brown.

Margaret comes from a long line of good cooks. She gets her talent from her mother, and her grandmother before her, who came to Asheville to work in a big hotel's kitchen after World War I. Margaret also got her curly black hair from her mother's side of the family; she has not cut it short like most women in their forties. Dan likes this. He likes the fact that his wife looks ten years younger than most of his friends' wives, or at least he used to notice things like that.

Right now Dan is with his mistress—his new car, a used Jaguar with fifty thousand miles on the odometer. He spends most of his free time driving recklessly around the neighborhood, trying not to run over the ducks that wander off the nearby golf course into the road. Dan and Margaret's house is just off Charlotte Street, across from the eighth hole. Most members of the country club are local royalty, old-money gentlemen who hack away at the sand traps while their new-money wives lounge by the pool. The groundskeeper is known for keeping aquatic fowl: mallards, geese, even five or six stately swans with clipped wings swim on the ponds amid all that immaculate green. But Dan has given up golf for the car; no longer content to loaf around with his clubs, now he wants the thrill of speed. Before the Jag, he drove a Honda Accord to the office and back, but last week he gave Margaret the Honda as an early anniversary present and bought himself the Jag. He goes for a drive every day after work. Margaret watches silently through the kitchen window over the sink, as he pulls out onto the street and guns the Jag toward the highway.

Margaret pulls out a long, sharp knife and slices open a plastic bag of dried figs. She begins to halve the fruits. The halves look like mummified lips; with each cut an ancient, lurid smile creeps out at her.

She pauses, the knife poised an inch above the cutting board. Today is her twenty-third wedding anniversary, and just now she is caught in a moment of reflection. Reading with her fingers the cuneiform of the wooden board, an artifact passed down from mother to daughter, Margaret moves back in time. She sees the spice caravans of Mesopotamia, the cradle of the dinner table—serpentine lines curving between the Tigris and Euphrates. Camels heavy-laden with saffron and thyme are sailing through the desert toward her and the other anxious wives waiting on the edge of Ur.

Sometimes Margaret wanders the Attic fish markets, far from the philosophers. She knows what they do not—logic breaks down on an empty stomach. Bearded men pry into the secrets of the heavens, but not one of them has invented a philosophy to teach us how to eat well. Prostitutes are moonlighting by the wharf, selling raw, bleeding tuna. The girls' complexions remind Margaret of spoiled oysters. Margaret pauses for a moment to feel the heft of the knife in her hand. Careful, careful. She could just as easily slice a finger in half with the Sabatier as a fig.

When Margaret daydreams, she never becomes someone else; rather, she recasts herself in similar roles in various settings. In Athens she is an aristocrat, her husband a powerful rhetorician. His funeral oration for their son has left the citizens numbed and dazed with grief. The entire city-state is in mourning. Not far from the market, merchant ships are slipping into the distance like old friends. The cold blue Aegean crashes on the coast.

Margaret and Dan's son, John, died four summers ago, drowned in the undertow off Cape Hatteras, where they had built a cabin in Rodanthe. John was only a few feet from shore, waving at his mother, when he was swept away. It took five days for the water to bring him back like a damaged letter, his body found by renters in the aftermath of a nor'easter. Waiting through the storm to look for John had been hard enough, but when he was found and Margaret wasn't allowed to see him, she became hysterical. The seventy-mile-per-hour winds and the violent surf had made the body endure terrible things. Dan had to force Margaret into the car to get off the island. She tasted sand all the way home.

"Damn." Margaret reprimands herself for not paying attention. She adjusts the gas under the wine, which has slipped from simmer into boil. The flames retract like cats' claws. Margaret smiles; she loves this stove. Gas allows for more precision than electric. The stove has a nineteenth-century cast-iron design, but the features are pure twenty-first: built-in griddle, two ovens, wok rings, six burners. Each burner is shaped like a star—eight radial fingers instead of the old, round eye. They provide even heat under the entire pan for fast searing or delicate simmering. The liquid settles. She places the figs in the pan—they blossom. Margaret preheats the oven.

In a few moments she makes her way to the refrigerator and fetches the duck. It has already been decapitated, plucked, and placed in a mesh net. Margaret makes short work of the net with a knife. Then she takes two bowls from the cabinet. One she fills with flour. Next to the stove are glass jars filled with staples:

bulk peppercorns, sugar, salt. She pours peppercorns into the Turkish coffee grinder. It is old, nobody knows how old; it's one of the items that made the trip across the Atlantic with Margaret's grandmother, all the way from Santorini, a Greek island in the Cyclades. The grinder is over a foot tall and made of solid brass; it is heavy with family mythology. Like the cutting board, it was given to her when she married. It is strong enough to crush bones into flour. Margaret grinds out four tablespoons of pepper.

The salt is low, so she reaches back into the cabinet. There is a little girl on the package, holding an umbrella in one hand and a cylinder of salt in the other. Margaret pours an equal amount of salt into the pepper bowl and then fills the glass container. Before she puts the salt away she examines the package again. On the box in the little girl's hands is another little girl, presumably holding salt. Margaret gets drunk trying to count all the little girls who live in her cabinet.

The duck's flesh is smooth, ugly, discolored like a newborn baby. Its cavity is filled with rich fat—duck butter, they call it. After dusting her right hand with flour, she begins to rip the duck butter out with her nails. While she does this, she tries to imagine how the recipe will look in print.

Chocolate Duck

DINNER FOR TWO

2 cups beef stock or canned beef broth

2 cups dry red wine

1 sixteen-ounce package of dried figs, halved

1 five- to seven-pound duck

1 orange, halved

1 large yellow onion, chopped

4 tbsp. salt

4 tbsp. pepper

4 bay leaves

6 tbsp. Armagnac or Hennessy cognac

3 tbsp. butter

3 ounces Ghirardelli or other quality semisweet chocolate, halved

Ducks were the first domesticated fowl. The Chinese kept them in little huts, like henhouses, over four thousand years ago. Maybe because of the birds' long history of domesticity, the Chinese say that eating duck keeps lovers faithful. There are recipes for roast duck in both the Ancient Greek cooking guide The Deipnosophist, *"The Banquette of the Wise," and in many of the household records of the Egyptian pharaohs. But it is in the medieval* Forme of Curey *that we find the definitive method. Duck should be stuffed with sweets: apples, raisins, prunes, quince, figs, sugar, and honey are all excellent ingredients for accenting the meat's rich flavor.*

After the invention of the printing press, the Forme of Curey *and other cooking guides were second only to the Bible in popularity. Newer editions of the guide had additional instructions if royalty were going to be at table. If serving duck to the king, a host might want to shred orange rind over the bird's skin, then pour a jigger or two of brandy on the platter and set it aflame.*

Of course, they didn't have chocolate in the Dark Ages, which is one of the reasons they were dark. . . .

"Well, there've been projects like this before," Ann H. Hardy had said on the phone a few months earlier. "Of course we'll give it a shot, but *The Ashevillian* had regionalism on its side, and that's really Southern Progress's bread and butter."

The Ashevillian was written in a matter of days soon after Margaret finished college. She entered UNC-Asheville after John died; Shakespeare seemed cheaper than psychoanalysis. She took twenty-one hours every semester and went summers. After graduation, she wrote poems filled with handsome drowned boys. At night John appeared to her in dreams, with his fair hair and wet blue eyes, dripping in his funeral suit. He described the grand civilizations under the ocean they could have seen together had she only caught his hand in time. She would write this all down in the morning, but when she was done her handwriting looked frail and pathetic. She never showed anyone.

Dan took to staying up drinking wine and brandy until long after his wife went to bed. He looked like Dan, acted like Dan, same big arms and shy smiles, but he ignored her. She persuaded him to come to bed early once, but when he complied it was as if John's corpse were under the sheets with them. Now Dan wanders around the house at odd hours of the night like a ghost, bumping into furniture.

She saw the ad in *Southern Living* for a first-cookbook contest and decided to write down the old recipes and her mother's stories about the wild life she'd led in Asheville. Margaret wrote about the time George Patton stayed in the hotel and showed her mother his ivory-handled .45s, and about Scott Fitzgerald's long nights at the bar when he came to visit Zelda in the loony bin. At the time, Asheville Asylum was one of the best in America; it occupied a nineteenth-century cobblestone mansion only a mile from Charlotte Street. The hotel and restaurant business was nothing if not interesting, but Margaret had never liked it much.

Her mother was rarely home (her father had died before she was born), and she was often alone.

The Ashevillian won the $1,000 prize and sold 10,000 copies in the Southeast alone. It was going into paperback, and the publisher gave her a $12,000 advance and a two-book deal. The first book had been easy, just a matter of turning her biography into recipes; but *Voyages of the Dinner Table* she had to research in the library and then conjure the rest up out of her imagination. It was exhausting, and she had to write with the additional burden of knowing that her editor wasn't overly enthusiastic about it.

Margaret cleans the duck fat from under her fingernails with a toothpick. In the back of *Voyages* she has compiled a *Did You Know?* list. Margaret never met a fact she didn't like. *Fact 31: Witches were said to smear cooked baby fat on their broom handles to give them the power of flight. Fact 32: In the sixteenth century, tobacco was often called the "dry drink" and was served after dinner in place of alcohol.* Margaret finds herself fatigued and wanting a cigarette, a habit she refuses to give up—there no longer seems to be a reason. But she will have to hold out until she gets the duck in the oven.

She begins massaging the mixture of salt and pepper into the bird's flesh, inside and out. She's a bit disgusted by the slickness of her hands, and she stops to wash them with steaming water and dishwashing liquid, but they won't come clean. She scrubs until it feels as if the meat will fall away from the bones, but her fingers are still sticky. She gives up.

She goes to the refrigerator again and takes out an onion and an orange. The orange is like its own little world, perfectly round, a reliable fact like the speed of light. Margaret remembers a lot of tidbits from high school. The Earth is approximately twenty-five thousand miles in circumference; to find the circumference of a circle, multiply the radius squared by pi. Margaret divides the orange at its equator. It falls apart. The problem with facts is that they are meaningless in and of themselves. A fact that stands alone is devoid of value; you have to understand the whole system of weights and pulleys to make one fact worth something. You always have to keep asking yourself *why*.

Margaret massages the duck with half of the orange. Dan is out there, on the road. He's wearing his aviator shades. The top is down. Maybe he's fighting his way around Black Mountain, or trying to find a long straightaway so he can get the Jag up to eighty, ninety, one hundred. He might even be risking his life trying to hug the sheer curves between here and Knoxville. That's where he went yesterday. Lately he has been taking the car farther and farther, as if he were an explorer preparing for a long expedition, testing the ship, testing his own endurance. Margaret milks the orange for its last drop of juice.

She puts the other hemisphere of orange inside the cavity of the duck. The fruit's puckered navel reminds her of maternity. She can recall every storybook she ever read to John. She finds it hard to remember what she did with herself before he was born. Dan had been a successful architect in Asheville for years before John's birth. They moved to Knoxville while Dan studied at the University of Tennessee, and she put him through school by waiting tables. She hated the work; he worshiped her for it because he knew it was a sacrifice, all those loveless soups and entrees meant for strangers. It made her feel like her mother, alone and sucking up to the public for tips.

Anonymity—that was one of the real difficulties in writing a cookbook. How do you cook for someone you've never shaken hands with, much less kissed or made love to? How do you put yourself into your food? That is the question. The Knoxville ordeal was soon over, and Dan got a good job. He designed the two-story Tudor they live in now with the massive kitchen just for her, the big house Margaret always wanted. And for a time this was enough.

Then came motherhood, which was frightening—not just the physicality of it, the moods, the cravings, the nausea (sometimes she still feels phantom pains of John's skull pushing into her spine), but the awesome, holy responsibility of it all. Baby John made her fear for her life when he nursed, that hungry, blind mouth gnawing at her breast. And when he slept, he slept so quietly. Children always seem like little strangers when they're sleeping, and this made Margaret feel like a pretender as a mother. She told Dan this once, and he laughed at her, but that was before the undertow. Even now Margaret doesn't think of John as dead. It seems more like he's asleep in another room of the house.

Through all this, neither Dan nor Margaret has ever mentioned divorce, and this has given her a little hope, though she can tell there's something sad and dangerous growing inside her husband, waiting to manifest itself. Something that stems from never having had the opportunity to say goodbye to their son, to weep over his body, to touch his little hand inside the coffin. Their lives are like the cabin in Rodanthe, which just sits there by the edge of the cold ocean, boarded up and haunted, waiting for the next hurricane.

Five months ago, the country club called. The greenskeeper ordered Margaret to come pick up her husband, who was drunk and causing a disturbance. Dan had clubbed a swan to death with a pitching wedge. By the time Margaret made it around the block, Dan had disappeared. Margaret didn't try to offer an explanation, and the greenskeeper didn't ask for one. He'd seen a lot of the world, and was a man not without pity. "Please, ma'am," he said. "Please. We can't have this. Keep him at home, whatever you have to do; don't let him come back. If he comes back, we'll have to press charges."

While Margaret minces the onion, she ponders the Middle Ages. Castles, cathedrals, flowing tapestries, knights fighting dragons. John used to tell her he thought a dragon lived inside Black Mountain. The dragon must be very old now, his ancient scales aching. He wishes a knight would come along and kill him; it would be indecorous to die of old age. Only he is afraid there are no knights left.

Even as a girl Margaret appreciated fine things, maybe because her mother never had many. Crystal, china, elegant platters—Margaret has a gift for pageantry, has mastered the art of arrangement. Always, after setting the table, she is overwhelmed by the heraldry of knives. There is something sublime about the way the silver glisters in the shadowy candlelight.

Tonight, after dinner, Dan and Margaret are going to a play. They are benefactors of the UNC-A theater, and they receive season tickets. Tonight's performance is *A Midsummer Night's Dream,* one of her favorites—the fairies are so courtly; the confusion is so well framed. But it's getting late, and Dan still isn't back.

Margaret wonders to what extent her life with Dan has been staged. Mother, father, wife, husband: the family just roles for half-hearted actors. After they built the golf course even the house didn't seem real; the country club turned the neighborhood into an amusement park. But Dan was happy because it increased the property values. Margaret thinks about all her friends who got divorced and moved west. Strangers live in their houses. Zelda Fitzgerald's grand asylum was turned into a real-estate office. It seems to Margaret, at forty-three, that even real estate isn't very real anymore. In a way, even John seems like an actor playing a corpse. For a moment she sees his body laid out across the kitchen table, surrounded by silver, his hands crossed under the candles.

Margaret puts the onion inside the duck with the orange and adds four bay leaves. The onion's vapor will make the duck succulent; the orange's sugar will caramelize and sweeten the onion. Margaret punctures the duck's flesh with a skewer and puts it in the oven. Everything is almost ready. Richard II's *Compound Sallet*, garnished with rose petals and marigolds, chills in the fridge, and *Beauvillier's Seventeenth-Century Cheese Soufflé* is on the counter. Cream almond pastries—darloy, or maids in waiting—are for dessert. In ten minutes Dan will either walk through the door with flowers or he won't come back at all. She sees his car smoldering on the side of the road, safety glass shattered like teeth around Dan's dead body. She wonders what she would do with his clothes.

Margaret drinks a glass of wine and smokes. The smoke makes her feel sad. She feels like Liz Taylor in *Butterfield 8* or Veronica Lake in *The Blue Dahlia*; she can only picture herself in sepia tones.

All that's left are the figs, cognac, and chocolate. The sauce has reduced to only a cup or so. Margaret pushes the movie out of her head and goes back to work. Over the sink she strains out the figs, which will be served on the side; she saves the rich liquid, returns it to the pan and pours in another glass of wine. With a wooden spoon she rubs the pan to deglaze the caramelized sugar on the sides. She walks into the living room, where Dan keeps the Hennessy behind the bar. This is what he drinks when he's up late. He thinks that just because it's expensive, he is a connoisseur and not a drunk.

She goes back into the kitchen and pours six tablespoons of the cognac into the sauce. Then she adds butter and flour to make it thicken. Now the final touch: the chocolate, semisweet gourmet chocolate. She eats a square. It makes her feel rich and bitter. The foil glimmers. Margaret picks up her knife to halve the wafers of chocolate before she adds them to the sauce. She is going to split the squares down the middle. On the cutting board she holds one between her forefinger and thumb.

Ahhh! the sorrow of a sliced thumb. Blood spills into the grooves of the board. The cut is deep. The knife so sharp, she keeps waiting for the pain. There is blood on her apron and on her dress. Blood glints on the foil. She sucks her thumb, and her mouth fills with copper.

She balls her fist and squeezes blood into the sauce. "For salt," she says aloud, and then begins to stir in the chocolate. When it has melted, the pan takes on rare depth. She is trying to find her image in the liquid. Instead she sees the Jag. Dan is driving toward the ocean, accelerating toward Hatteras, the abandoned cabin, and the undertow. She knows she should be running for the bathroom—for gauze, a towel, *something*—but she doesn't. The whole universe swirls about the blue flames of the stove.

By the time she picks up the legal pad and the grease pencil, she has already composed the recipe in her head. She writes with purpose, knows as the pencil graces the page that the prose is succinct, clear, flawless. She will show them; before she is done she will show the interns and strangers in the test kitchen a recipe fit for kings. She will give them the recipe for swan.

This has been simmering in her head for a while, ever since Dan brought home the great white swan he slaughtered. It was a long time before he came back to the house that day. Margaret sat in the kitchen for hours, waiting. She was horrified when he lurched in cradling the enormous bird. The greenskeeper hadn't told her that Dan wouldn't let it go, that he'd been holding it all the time they were on the phone.

When Dan walked in, there was blood on his shirt, and somehow there was even blood in his hair. He sat down on the floor like a little kid with the bird in his lap and wept. Margaret knelt beside him and cried too. The swan's beak was crushed; its broken neck dangled straight down. It had bright eyes. She had not known swans were so large. Then she made a mistake; she tried to take it away from him. For a long time they struggled on the floor. But he held on, clutching the bird to his chest with his big arms, refusing to give it up. In the end there was just no way Margaret could take it away from him, and there was just no way he was letting go.

Report from Junction

Late in the afternoon Kurt Schaffer rides on his roan gelding up to his uncle Pleasant's feed store, only to find that the old man has already left for the hospital in Johnson City, to visit his sick wife. Kurt doesn't much care for filling in at the feed store. The public life of a merchant doesn't appeal to him. He prefers the solitary existence of working cattle on his father's ranch, or the excitement of playing football on the weekends. Working at the store means that he can become locked into pointless conversations; he's at the mercy of any son of a bitch with six bits for a bag of Ripsnorter sweet feed.

The feed store is only a mile or so away from the abandoned courthouse in Blanco. The county seat moved to Johnson City years ago. The year is 1954 and the Blanco River is dry. All of Texas is four years into a drought that has caused everything that was once green to turn brown, curl up, and blow away. The only vegetation that remains consists of a few mesquite trees, honey locust, and oceans of short cactus. Kurt will be a sophomore at Texas A&M before rain falls on his home again. That same year the Aggies will win their first Southwest Conference championship in fifteen years. But right now Kurt is beginning his last year of high school, and the Aggies are perennial losers. Even so, he has heard rumors that things are about to change for A&M. The newspaper reported last week that the new head coach, Paul "Bear" Bryant, is determined to institute an extreme brand of spartan military discipline.

Nine days ago Bryant drove his new team deep into the desert, to a place called Junction, where the team has been housed in abandoned military barracks. The players practice all day in a field of sand and clay drawn off in chalk lines, and they tackle one another atop jagged rocks and prickly pears. Denied water for hours at a time, the team continues to run and block and tackle no matter what. The boys carry on with sprained knees, dislocated shoulders, broken noses, broken ribs. According to the newspaper, hardly a man among them is still whole.

A syndicated columnist uses words like "bone-crushing" and "inhumane." He describes the players as "bloody" and "mangled" and compares them to soldiers on the Bataan Death March or to concentration-camp victims. Two days ago one of the players, Drake Goetze, a center from Paris, fell out with heatstroke and almost died. Pushed beyond their endurance, other members of the team have simply fled, sneaking out of the ovenlike Quonset huts in the middle of the night to hitchhike away. Every day the reporter phones in an update on the gruesome situation and shames the quitters by publishing a list with their names in bold type. Originally one hundred and eleven players, the team has been reduced to around forty, and still the practice continues. Kurt vows to himself that next year, when his time comes to ride out into the desert, his name will not be printed in such a list. By the time he finishes next year's training camp under this new slave-driving coach, his daddy's ranch will have gone under, and maybe his uncle's feed store, too. His aunt April will probably be dead, and his family may well have moved away from their home in Blanco County forever. At any rate Kurt will not quit, because he will have nothing to go back to.

T-Willy, Uncle Pleas's World War I buddy, walks out from the shadowy doorway onto the porch of the feed store as Kurt ties his horse to one of the support beams. "Kurt, where in the heck have you been? Pleas was expecting you an hour ago."

Kurt isn't in the mood to be talked down to, especially by the likes of T-Willy. Kurt has spent the entire morning riding fence, and he's tired and disgusted. He goes about the business of unsaddling the roan without so much as a hello. Kurt needs help, but he won't ask for it. The horse stepped on his left hand a few days ago, and the last three fingers are broken and taped together, the nails black and split. Kurt has always been a little suspicious of T-Willy, partly because the old man's a half-breed: part German, part Mexican. But mostly Kurt dislikes T-Willy because he's never seen the old man do a hard day's work. He just sits here in the feed store with the fans on him, drinking whiskey, smoking cigarettes, and playing checkers with Pleas, living off the skinny tit of a soldier's pension. Instead of asking for the old man's aid, Kurt grips the saddle horn tightly with his thumb and forefinger and manages to drag the saddle down off the horse's back without dropping it.

"You know I'm too down in my back to load up anybody's truck. I don't even know how to open up that cash register in there."

"Everybody pays with credit anyway," Kurt says. "Has anybody been in today?"

"Not since Pleas left."

"Well, then, it hasn't been a problem, now has it?"

"You worried Pleas. That's the damn problem. He doesn't need any more of that."

Kurt lays the saddle on the railing of the porch and then drapes a froth-soaked blanket matted with horsehair next to it. A saddle-shaped sweat outline on the gelding's back is already beginning to evaporate in the sun. Next Kurt takes his father's .45-caliber cavalry revolver out of his jeans and places it in the saddle-bag in exchange for a pick, which he will use to clean the rocks and dung out of the horse's hooves. Every morning for the past two years Kurt has risen well before sunrise, put on his work clothes and a baseball cap, saddled up the roan, and ridden five or ten miles around the perimeter of his daddy's property. He carries the .45 in order to put water-starved cattle out of their misery. He has killed dozens since the beginning of the long, cruel summer—so many that he has begun to think of himself as the ranch's executioner, a kind of resident Angel of Death bringing peace to all the wretched animals the land will not support. And the job is getting to him.

Last week was the worst. Riding across the northeast corner of the ranch, Kurt spotted a pack of turkey buzzards wheeling in the cloudless morning light. He figured they were circling more dead cattle. But as he came closer, he could see that the head of one of his daddy's prostrate Herefords was still moving; the animal was beating itself senseless in the dust. Kurt kicked the gelding and charged up to a gruesome sight: unwilling to wait for death, the buzzards had just picked out the Hereford's eyes. Two or three of the birds bobbled with the strewn, sticky nerves; the others tapped their beaks into the hollow sockets of the Hereford's skull. Kurt unloaded the pistol, killing one buzzard on the ground and two others in midair before the reports chased the rest out of range.

"Take off, you sons a bitches!" Kurt screamed, pointing the empty gun up in the air. Then he got off the horse and looked down at the savaged remains of the cow. The cow stared blindly at him out of one of the upturned holes in her skull. The other side of her face she rubbed violently on the ground, her black tongue caking with dust. Kurt cursed himself for continuing to shoot after the buzzards were out of range. He had to reload in order to put the tortured Hereford out of her misery.

Nervous, the horse turned its hindquarters away from Kurt as he snatched up the reins. Kurt stuck the gun in his jeans so that he could fiddle around in the saddlebag while the horse's backside continued to drift away from him. Kurt jerked down hard on the reins to stop the horse from moving; the bit clenched against the roan's jaw, scaring him still. The horse laid his ears flat back on his head and shivered. It seemed to take forever for Kurt to find the box of shells. When he finally did, he let go of the reins, drew the gun, and fumbled with the pin that released the revolver's chamber. He dropped both the gun and the box of shells, and the bullets spilled out on the ground. Kurt fell to his knees and lurched for the revolver with his right hand. The ammunition rolled between the fetlocks of the roan. Without thinking, Kurt extended his hand, and the nervous roan stepped backward in retreat. The horse's front hoof landed squarely on Kurt's fingers. For a hellish moment the hand was simply stuck under the horse, and there was nothing Kurt could do to move it. The horse could have easily reared up and trampled him to death or turned and kicked Kurt in the head with one of his powerful back legs. All Kurt could do was stare at his crushed hand pinned to the ground, and think to himself, *Oh, my God. She is still alive. She is still alive.*

Kurt replays the bloody scene with the buzzards over and over in his brain as he lifts up one leg of the roan and scrapes debris out of the V-shaped groove in its hoof.

"Goddamn," T-Willy says, trying to start up the conversation again. "I do believe this drought is rougher than the one in the thirties. If it don't rain soon, every rancher from Austin to New Mexico will be broke."

"You reckon?" Kurt asks, rolling his eyes. Now that he is here to keep an eye on the store, he wishes the old man would go away. Kurt knows as well as anyone what's going to happen to the ranchers from Austin to New Mexico. It will only be a matter of months before his own daddy goes under, and when enough people like Kurt's daddy go broke, his uncle's feed store will go broke, and the banks will take everything.

The day Kurt shot the Hereford, he returned home from his morning ride to eat breakfast. Instead of eating, he poured himself a cup of coffee and went outside on the front porch to drink it. His father rose from the kitchen table, where he had been picking at a mixture of eggs and hog brains, and followed. Kurt had already wrapped his fingers in a blue bandana.

"What happened to your hand, boy?"

Kurt hesitated only a moment before he told his father the story of the buzzards' monstrous attack. He almost cried when he came to the part about having to wait on the roan to release his hand. "It was stupid. Plain old stupid."

"I want you to know something, Kurt," his father said. "Something no one else knows yet. When you move off to College Station in the fall, I'm selling everything but the goats." Kurt's father seized his shoulder so hard that the boy almost dropped his coffee cup. "You're old enough to be on your own now, Kurt. Don't screw up your scholarship, son, because from here on out you're going to have to be responsible for yourself." His father lowered his gaze. "I'm sorry, I had to say that."

Kurt keeps his back to T-Willy as he grooms the gelding. He doesn't need a shiftless old man to tell him about hard times. "Why don't you try giving your mouth a rest for a little while," he says.

"Kurt, I'll swan," T-Willy says, scratching his curly gray head in wonder. "You are the aggravatinest thing I ever run across." He sits down in a rocking chair. "I hope somebody pops that fresh mouth of yours for you when you go off to school next year." The old man starts rolling a cigarette. It's not a pretty sight. First he takes his teeth out and sets them in his lap. After he has rolled up the tobacco, his wormy tongue peeks out of its toothless cave to seal the paper.

Kurt hates the idea of getting old. He runs his left hand up the buttons of his chambray work shirt and scratches his stomach, which is flat and hard, though a little black pit of fear rests under the muscles. His only physical imperfection is a scar under his left eye, a white star puncture wound, a memento from Kurt's childhood when he fell off a Shetland pony and landed face first on a barbed wire fence. His coordination is better now; he has power and agility.

Kurt is tough and mean, but a bit of a runt. Because he works so hard on the ranch, he can't keep weight on. At 165 pounds, he is really too light to play college ball; A&M was one of the few major universities that offered him a scholarship. Jess Neely, at Rice, made him an offer, but the ties and jackets that Rice students have to wear to class are expensive. A military institute, Texas A&M provides uniforms. But if the news reports from Junction are true, Kurt will most likely get bounced around pretty good when his turn comes to practice in the desert, and he wonders if he has made the wrong decision. He will never have the luxury of backing down from a fight, or even the chance to rise casually from a pileup. He must never allow himself to dog it, not even a little, when running the gassers or playing bull-in-the-ring. Kurt must positively shine with hustle and aggression if he hopes to win a position; otherwise, he will find himself riding the pine in the fall, and will maybe lose the chance to renew the scholarship.

"You have to act like a banty rooster." This is what his father, who is fond of cockfighting and boxing metaphors, tells him. "Half the size but twice as mean. That's you, Kurt." Sometimes before a tough game Kurt likes to hop himself up on white cross and bennies, cheap trucker speed that makes his brain itch and his teeth ache, but the pills keep him immune to fatigue or pain. Now he is so tired from working on the ranch that he wishes he had something with a little pep to keep him going. Then Kurt remembers that T-Willy usually carries more-soothing medicine.

"T-Willy, you got your bottle on you?"

T-Willy looks sideways, like he's thinking about holding a

grudge, but then he grins, reaches into his overalls, and hands the kid the bottle. "Take it easy on that stuff."

Kurt takes a mighty swig from the bottle. It doesn't taste like whiskey—more like sweet wine—but it's still hot and strong like liquor. "Damn, what is this?" he says.

"They call it peach beer. It's brandy made with peach peels. My cousin sent it to me from Georgia. Ain't it smooth?"

Kurt grunts and takes another slug.

"Here, you best hand that back. Here comes your uncle. He'll have my hide if he knows I'm getting you drunk."

Kurt hands the bottle back as he spies a green Ford speeding toward the feed store from Johnson City. But it's going much too fast to be Kurt's uncle, a cautious driver who rarely gets above fifty miles an hour. As the truck comes closer to the store, Kurt can see that it is similar to his uncle's but much newer; even through all the dust the chrome trim glimmers. T-Willy finishes his cigarette and replaces his teeth.

The truck pulls into the drive, runs right up next to the roan, and parks. Straight off Kurt is sore with the driver, who doesn't think enough of his horse to park a few yards away. If the roan weren't gelded, it might have gotten nervous and reared up and possibly fallen over and hurt itself. More likely, it would have kicked the shit out of the shiny new truck and split a hoof. But the roan is tired too, so it simply pulls back on its halter and gives a shivering nicker. Kurt doesn't recognize the driver, which means he must be from pretty far off. When he steps out, Kurt sees that he's a big man, well over six feet tall and thick in the middle. He has a red moustache, and he's wearing an expensive Stetson, and a denim work shirt that is altogether too clean. A little blonde girl in pigtails, no more than seven and wearing brown overalls, jumps out of the passenger seat. The wind shifts, and even before the stranger has slammed the door of his truck, Kurt can smell that they have brought something with them, something that has been in the sun too long.

T-Willy, delighted to see the little girl, hunkers down in his chair and says, "Hey there, cowgirl, who you got there with you?"

"My daddy," she says, with an adult seriousness. Then she moves behind her father, so that she is difficult to see.

The man with the red moustache gives T-Willy an apologetic look and then turns to Kurt. "Pleas ain't here, is he?"

"Nope." Kurt shakes his head. "He's in Johnson City."

The stranger looks disappointed. "Would you mind coming over here and looking at something for me?"

Kurt and T-Willy exchange looks; then Kurt nods and walks to the back of the truck. The man lowers the tailgate, frowning. On top of a bed of canvas fertilizer sacks lies a newborn Red Angus bull, no more than a day or two old, and by the looks of it, the calf has spent a considerable amount of that time suffering out in the heat. It hasn't been licked clean. Dried afterbirth has crusted around its eyes and nostrils; its hide is matted with dried blood. Its nose is dull and pink. Already, flies are gathering around the calf, lighting near its eyes and in the folds of its nostrils and on the umbilical cord. It is so tiny that it looks more like an orphaned fawn than a calf. The bull breathes slowly, dehydrated, too weak to even lift its head.

The little girl climbs on top of the back wheel and stands on tiptoes so that she can peer over into the bed and get a closer look. She smiles at Kurt. "His name is Chester."

The father turns to Kurt. "I can't figure why his momma don't want him. I guess it just happens that way sometimes."

"Lack of water," T-Willy offers. "It does things to their head. Makes cows plumb crazy. Or it might have been her first one and she didn't know what to do with it. That happens too."

"Look, my cousin's the cattleman, but he left town this morning. I just found this little fellow laying out near some brush not far from the house. I don't really know what to do with him. Somebody told me you can buy powdered milk here. Is that true?"

Kurt nods and walks up onto the porch and through the dark doorway of the store. He is almost bowled over by the rich smell of corn, oats, and molasses. He moves past stacks of crushed hay and cracked-corn feed, past the protein pellets and a pyramid of red salt blocks, all the way to the back of the store, where a few fifty-pound bags of powdered milk are stacked atop one another. Kurt selects one marked "Milk Starter"; it contains colostrum— the first milk a cow gives after birth, a thin, yellowish fluid full of minerals. Other bags are marked "Milk Replacer"—the hind milk, the white milk.

Both the milk starter and the milk replacer are old. Since the drought most people don't bother trying to save an individual calf. Kurt shoulders the sack of colostrum and grabs a liter milk bottle off the shelf. The milk bottle is equipped with a long, vulgar-looking three-inch nipple that resembles a little boy's penis, pink and stiff. While Kurt is working in the back, he can barely make out the conversation T-Willy is having with the little girl's father. The man's name is something-or-other Dougan or Cougan, and he is an oilman, an executive, from Houston. But his relations live here in Blanco County. Walking back toward the doorway Kurt clearly hears the oilman say, "My cousin Bill wants me to buy in on his ranch, so I came to check the place out."

Kurt finds himself wishing that his father had some rich relatives, but his relatives are no different from himself, third- or fourth-generation Krauts, here from the time when Texas was still a part of Mexico.

Before Kurt can get back outside, T-Willy starts running his mouth about Aunt April, gossiping about her diabetic stroke, her blindness, how in all likelihood the doctors will have to amputate her legs, things he shouldn't speak about with strangers—with anyone. When Kurt gets out the door, he interrupts the conversation. "Here you go," he says, throwing the powdered milk onto the tailgate and setting the milk bottle on top of it.

"Mr. Cougan here is thinking about buying into Bill Worley's operation," T-Willy says. "They're cousins."

"Is that so?" Kurt says, not really asking. "You want me to show you how this works?"

"I'd appreciate that." Cougan tips his hat, cowboy style.

The little girl, still standing on the Ford's back tire, starts bouncing up and down, rocking the bed of the truck. She's so excited that Kurt can't help smirking. The poor girl must have lived all her life in the city.

Kurt pulls the drawstring on the powdered-milk sack and then steps up into the truck, seizes the tiny bull by the ears, and drags him to the tailgate. Cougan's daughter jumps off her tire and runs to the back of the truck so that she can watch what is about to take place. Kurt unscrews the nipple on the giant baby bottle and scoops about a cup of formula into the thick glass.

"What happened to your fingers?" Cougan's daughter is staring at the mess attached to his left hand.

"Damn, Katharine, that ain't polite."

For the first time all day Kurt laughs. "That's okay. She's just curious." But Kurt is unwilling to tell the real story behind his broken fingers, so he says, "Playing football."

"Football?" Cougan's eyes brighten. "You Kurt Schaffer?"

Kurt nods.

"You gonna be a redshirt Aggie next year?"

"Yep."

"Shoot, boy, I hope you're ready for one tough season. I hear that Bryant fellow works his players into the ground. He did it at Kentucky, too. That's why the Aggies got him. But from the way people talk, shit, he'll be lucky if he don't end up killing somebody. I read in the newspaper he's run off all but thirty-six men. You know, that boy from Paris is still in the hospital. If Bryant don't take those boys home soon, he won't have enough players left to field a team."

"Can we feed Chester now?" Katharine asks, impatient.

Kurt hands the milk bottle with the yellow powder in it to Katharine. "There's a bathroom inside the store. Go past the cash register, past the horse tack and harness, and turn right. Can you fill this up with hot water for me?"

Katharine says she can.

"Run the tap till it gets real hot, okay?" Kurt turns to Cougan. "Do you still have that newspaper on you?"

Cougan retrieves the local paper from the truck cab and hands it to Kurt. Kurt turns to the sports section and scans the headlines until he finds "Report from Junction," by Allen Wier. The article recounts yet another hellish practice, a day full of blood and sand. At one point Wier describes a confrontation between Bryant and the father of Drake Goetze, the heatstroke victim from Paris. Goetze's parents had come to collect their son from the Junction infirmary. Because of his weak heart, they have demanded that Goetze never play another down of football. The article ends with a brief interview with the coach, in which Bryant's only comment on the matter is, "If a boy is a quitter, I want to find out about it now, not in the fourth quarter." Then comes the list of four new names. Goetze's is among them, and this makes Kurt angry. If the boy had died on the practice field, would the papers have called him a quitter then, too? Kurt lowers the paper and looks at the bloody, flop-eared calf shivering in the sun, drawing flies.

He picks up the long pink nipple and pinches the tip. A tiny hole opens up through the thick rubber. "Those bastards at whatever factory makes these things should be shot. You leave it like this and the poor calf just winds up sucking air. Hey, T-Willy, you got your pocketknife on you?"

"Uh-huh."

"Toss it here."

Kurt catches the knife with his right hand and flicks open the blade. Cougan watches him curiously as Kurt slashes a little X into the top of the nipple and then inserts the tip of the blade into the tiny hole, coring it out. When Katharine returns, Kurt takes the bottle away from her, caps it, and shakes vigorously. Sitting down next to the calf, he grabs it by the neck and allows some of the colostrum to dribble onto the calf's tongue. Blackish placenta smears across the young man's shirt as he slips the nipple into the calf's mouth. The calf gags and regurgitates the milk into Kurt's lap. Soaked, Kurt smells like a mixture of chalk and eggs. He curses.

"You think he's too far gone?" Cougan asks.

"Nope. He just don't know how to suck yet. He'll get a taste for it in a second."

Kurt dribbles more of the milk into the calf's mouth. Instead of trying to make the calf nurse the bottle, he massages its throat, forcing it to swallow. He does this three times, and after the third attempt the calf gives a guttural cough as the milk slides down. Kurt puts the little bull in a headlock in order to keep its head elevated, and this time the calf offers a blind attack on the nipple, eventually sucking the milk.

When Kurt was a kid, before powdered milk and baby bottles were made for livestock, if a momma cow ever abandoned her calf, Kurt's grandfather would milk another cow, mix that milk with a raw egg, and use a kitchen funnel to pour the enriched liquid into a drenching bottle. A drenching bottle looked like a wine bottle but had a much longer neck. The old man would have Kurt tie a rope around the calf's neck and throw it over a rafter in order to elevate the calf's head. Then Kurt's grandfather would stick the long glass neck of the drenching bottle into the calf's mouth and down its throat, forcing it to swallow the thick milk.

It makes Kurt feel good to think about the days when his grandfather was still around, and everything was glistening and green as far as the eye could see. Kurt hugs the nursing calf in the headlock for quite a while. The little bull rubs its body up against the boy as he daydreams. Eventually the calf finds strength enough to bob its head a little, as if it were punching its mother's udder.

Kurt grins and pulls the bottle away. Katharine looks on in amazement. "Can I feed him?" she asks.

"Sure." Kurt nods, and asks her father to put her up on the tailgate. Kurt hands her the bottle. She stands on the tailgate, holding the bottle outward. Milk drips near her feet as Kurt picks up the calf and holds its face to the streaming nipple. Kurt starts to tell the little girl to tilt the bottle up high, so that the calf won't have any problem swallowing. Then he feels something move through the fingers on his good hand. He looks down to find several translucent worms, less than a quarter of an inch long, working their way through the caked-up corner of the calf's right eye. Kurt pulls the calf away from the nipple, flips it on its side, and brushes its eyes clean just in time to spot more maggots boiling up from the pink sores behind the eyelashes.

"Oh, hell."

"What's the matter?" Cougan asks.

"Man, your bull here's got the screwworms." Even when things were green, screwworms had been a problem for newborns. Screwworms are the larvae of blue-bellied blowflies, which lay their eggs in the wounded flesh of living animals. Kurt knows that some of the worms have probably already burrowed deep into the calf's body, and soon they will screw themselves into its vital organs and suck the life right out of it. In fact, with worms already on the calf's head, the maggots will most likely screw themselves into its brain and drive it completely mad before they exit back through its eyes. Kurt has never seen flies blow into the eyes before, although he has heard that they can blow inside the nose. Usually the flies lay their eggs in the navel of a newborn. This can be easily treated by mixing kerosene and lard into a balm and applying it to the stomach. The kerosene kills the worms while the lard holds the chemical solution in place. But Kurt quickly realizes that putting kerosene on the sores around the calf's eyes will blind it.

"Look, uh, Mr. Cougan." Kurt weighs his words carefully, not wanting to upset the little girl. "You best leave Chester here with me. It'll probably be better if I take care of him myself."

"But, Daddy, you promised—you promised I could take care

of him," the girl begs. "We need to take Chester back to Uncle Bill's with us. Please."

Cougan's eyes dart back and forth between Kurt and his daughter. "Actually, son, she's right. It ain't my calf to leave. It's my cousin's. He'll know what to do with him."

T-Willy attempts to intercede in Kurt's behalf. "I don't think you understand what the boy here is saying. That calf is in a lot of pain. It ain't going to get much better."

Cougan's eyes are fixed on Katharine, who is on the verge of tears.

Kurt lays the calf's head down on the tailgate to rest. "I'm telling you he's done for," he says. "There ain't no sense in dragging it out."

That does it. Katharine's face goes down into her hands, and she sobs.

Cougan puts his arm around her and cuts Kurt an evil look. "Well, son, why don't you let me be the judge of that." Then he whispers down to his daughter, "It's all right, honey. We'll take Chester home to Uncle Bill." Cougan cuddles the little girl, gently pressing her face into the swell of his broad stomach.

Kurt glances at the calf. The poor creature is shaking in pain, unable even to lick the yellow regurgitated milk off its nose. Kurt turns back to the rich oilman and his weeping daughter, her tears the only stain on his crisp, clean shirt. "Why, you silly son of a bitch."

Katharine stops crying. T-Willy winces. Cougan's expression of paternal sympathy shatters. "Katharine, get in the truck," he says. She knows better than to argue. She slowly climbs down off the tailgate and lets herself into the Ford. Cougan waits until she has closed the door. "Now, why don't you get off my truck, you little shit."

Kurt knows that as soon as he steps off the tailgate the oilman will swing at him. So he moves back and bounds in an athletic flash over the right side of the truck, hoping the roan won't decide to kick him as he flies through the air. The horse nickers and pulls back against its halter, as it did when Cougan drove up.

Already Cougan is stalking around the opposite side of the truck, fists balled for action. "Look, son, I'm going to show you not to cuss me in front of my girl." T-Willy puts a hand on Cougan's shoulders in an effort to calm him, but Cougan bats it down, knocking the thin old man to the ground. This gives Kurt just the time he needs to make it to the saddlebag and draw the .45. Cougan's eyes go flat with fear and hate as the boy turns the gun on him. For just a moment Kurt prays that the man will keep coming. He would love to shoot Cougan in his fat gut, watch all that good food and smugness spill onto the dirt. How much different could it be from easing the dumb suffering of a steer mad for water or a fevered calf with worms itching through its brain? He has done it dozens of times—the quick flick of the hammer, and then the mark of the dime-sized hole, and then a little peace for everyone. All the past there ever was, all the future there is ever going to be, meet at this place and fold into a single moment—the pulling of the trigger. Kurt is exhilarated by the fact that he suddenly has the power to change his life, and he keeps the gun leveled as he tries to figure out if he should.

Jail, Kurt thinks, might even be a relief: no hellish football camps out in the desert, no land auctions to witness. No winners, no losers, just a small, dark cell with plenty of cool water to drink.

But then Kurt's mind turns back to the ugly turkey buzzards blinding the Hereford, picking and picking their way through life. The murderous moment slips away from him.

Apparently Cougan has also surmised that Kurt isn't going to shoot him. He continues to advance. Cougan's face is puffy and red with hate, and Kurt wonders if he will still go to jail if he doesn't shoot but the oilman dies of a heart attack. Kurt decides to bluff. He cocks the hammer and yells something he heard in a roadhouse once, when one of his friends wanted to scare a big Yankee from Cleveland out of a fight. "Mr. Cougan, I'm just a little old country boy. But I'll clue you, I'm mean as hell." As soon as the words leave his mouth they seem stupid and frail, the threat of a hick, and Cougan is coming on as if he has heard nothing at all.

Kurt can think of only one thing to do. He swings the gun away from Cougan and points it toward the child in the truck.

"No!" Cougan cries. He stops long enough to look at his daughter. Katharine's face is pressed in horror against the window of the Ford. She doesn't have sense enough to duck under the dash. Instead she screams, "Daddy, Daddy!"

"No, please." The sight of his frightened daughter takes all the fight out of Cougan. He backs down, slides his body along the hood of the truck, and slowly makes a retreat to the other side. Kurt follows him halfway, keeping the gun pointed at the little girl until he backs up the porch steps. T-Willy has managed to get inside the feed store and is peering out the dark window.

Cougan opens the door of the Ford. "This ain't over," he says. "I'll kill you for this." Kurt points the gun back toward the oilman and keeps it on him in case he has a pistol of his own under the seat of the truck or in the glove compartment. But Kurt is pretty sure that Cougan won't risk any shooting with his daughter next to him in the cab. Cougan pushes his little girl down in her seat and peels out in reverse, his ruddy face receding into a cloud of dust. But he floods the engine, and the truck stalls. Kurt raises the .45 again.

After two or three tries Cougan manages to turn the engine over. He shifts into first and floors the accelerator. The Ford lurches forward, violently flinging the little bull off the tailgate and onto the ground. The bottle shatters. The calf is too weak to cry out and lands in the dirt with a thud, as if it were already dead. When he sees this, rage wells up in Kurt all over again, and he is tempted to try to shoot out the truck's tires. But a little voice inside his head tells him to leave well enough alone. T-Willy comes back onto the porch, and they watch together as the green Ford disappears, a line of powdered milk running all the way to the highway.

"Kurt, I'm afraid you're out of your damn mind," T-Willy says, as he shrugs at Kurt and starts walking toward the calf. It lies lifeless, like a blown-out tire next to the road.

"You reckon?" Kurt asks, swinging the cocked gun in the direction of the old man. T-Willy puts up his hands. They stay that way for a second or two, and then Kurt unloads four rounds, not into the old man but into the calf—two in the belly, two in the skull. As he lowers the gun, Kurt feels a wave of regret wash over him. He is sorry that he pointed the gun at his uncle's friend, and thinking about pointing the gun at the little girl makes him feel sick at his cowardice. He even feels sorry he had to kill the calf with the screwworms twisting in its eyes, but mostly Kurt feels sorry for himself, because he knows that for all his trouble, his life hasn't changed a bit, and in the morning he will have to get up out of bed and put on his work clothes and saddle the roan, and the whole thing will start over again.

Chickensnake

Somehow the chickensnake had managed to climb up the twenty-foot steel pole and into one of the hollowed-out gourds the farmers had hung there as birdhouses for purple martins. Now the snake was coiled up around an empty nest, hugging it as if to keep it warm. Only the chickensnake's head stuck out into the world, as if the snake itself were frozen in the process of hatching from the shell of an egg, but every so often it would taste the air with its tongue to show it was still alive. The snake had lowered the clear membranes across its eyes and had puffed the glistening scales along the back of its neck to catch the last of the fleeting sunlight. Being deaf, the snake paid no mind to the flock of fussy birds screeching about its head, somersaulting left and right, swooping toward the snake's slightly upturned nose yet never daring to touch it. For the first time ever, the chickensnake was on top of the world, looking down.

Below, Hazel Trull was backing the three-quarter-ton truck up to the mouth of the old barn when he noticed the martins. "Look over there," Haze said to his father, pointing to the storm of birds turning circles around their homes.

Haze's daddy stepped out of the passenger side. "I wonder what they're so upset about?"

The martins weren't mere pets or yard decoration. Like the cats that moused the barn, they earned their keep. One martin could eat its body weight in mosquitoes in a single day, and often picked off tobacco worms and cut worms that devoured the tomatoes and corn. But it was hard not to feel a certain gratitude toward the martins' beauty. When the sunlight caught them just right, their black feathers took on a purple sheen, like fresh transmission fluid or wine. Haze and his daddy walked to the back of the barn to get a closer look.

It was August and Haze's daddy was wearing a long-sleeved work shirt to protect him from the nettles in the square bales of fescue the two were hauling out of the field. There had been a drought for much of the summer, and the bales were light, scraggly, and coarse. Against his father's warning, Haze had discarded his own long-sleeved shirt and White Mule work gloves in hopes of getting some relief from the near hundred-degree heat. Now his bare arms were cut up and his hands blistered. He would have put them back on if his daddy weren't so quick to say "I told you so." Ever since Wayne, Haze's older brother, had died in the spring, Haze's father had been watching him like a new mother cow, never letting him out of his sight. No longer was Haze allowed to go walking in the woods alone or swimming with his friends down at the channel. When Haze's daddy wasn't farming, he was the Kennedy High School principal. When Haze entered the seventh grade next fall, it was going to be like baling hay all year long, one "I told you so" after another.

Without Wayne there to help out, Haze was having to do all the ground work himself. Drive the truck, hop out, throw a bale of hay into the bed, run around the other side, toss up another bale, get back behind the wheel and drive across another terrace, then start all over again. Haze's daddy stood in the back of the truck silently stacking the bales into a tight pyramid, occasionally telling Haze, "You need to get a move on, the sky's going to open up on us." They were racing the storm clouds already on the horizon. After a two-month drought, the weatherman had surprised everyone by predicting thunderstorms in the afternoon. If the hay got wet out in the field, it would mildew and turn sorry when put into storage. Haze's uncle Poochie had said he was going to take a half-day off work to help out, but it was almost dinnertime and he was late.

Haze's daddy was the first to spot the chickensnake. "I ain't believing this," he said, pointing toward one of the gourds on the right. "Look." At the top of the pole, under the wheeling birds, was a crisscross of planks. Ten gray gourds hung from each plank, five on either side of the pole. With the last of the sun still shining bright, it took a moment for Haze's eyes to adjust, but then there it was—the evil-looking head of the snake protruding from the second gourd on the right.

"How do you reckon he got up there?" Haze asked.

"Climbed, I guess."

"Can a snake climb straight up a steel pole? I would have thought it'd be too slick." Haze knew that snakes used their scales for traction, but they needed something to grab on to. Haze had once seen a man on television lay a timber rattler down on a large pane of glass. The reptile had become helpless and just flopped around.

"Evidently, this ain't your everyday snake."

"Chickensnake?"

Haze's daddy nodded. Chickensnakes were fond of creeping into barns and henhouses to eat eggs. A big one could swallow whole chicks. But there had been no chickens on the farm for years, not since Haze's grandfather, Lonzo Trull, had passed away. He used to keep banty hens in one of the old mule stalls in the barn, but after he died Haze's daddy sold the hens. "I've already seen the cats kill two little ones this year," said Haze. "I wonder where they're coming from. There must be a bed of them around here someplace."

"Yeah, well this must be the daddy. Go into the house and fetch your gun."

Haze made his way across the gravel drive, onto the front porch, and then down into his parents' bedroom. He took down the little .22-caliber Remington bolt action from the gun cabinet, then grabbed a handful of shells from a candy dish at the top of the case. Haze hadn't touched the rifle in weeks, not since Wayne had been shot in a hunting accident. Wayne was killed by Mr. Parker, a seventy-five-year-old neighbor who'd been a childhood friend of Haze's grandfather, and so he had always had an open invitation to hunt on their property. Mr. Parker had shot Wayne in the face with a 12-gauge shotgun at close range. Ten years ago the old man had become eligible to purchase a lifetime hunting license for $50.75, and no one had bothered to check up on him afterward. At the hearing, the old man had admitted he was "confused" when he shot Wayne, even though he understood that

Wayne was not a deer or turkey. Mr. Parker was a World War II veteran, and there was no telling what kind of electrical storm had boomed through his brain when he killed Wayne.

Touching the Remington, once again Haze imagined how it must have happened. First he sees Wayne's balloon-like face, his gray-blue eyes peering out from under his baseball cap. His brother wasn't handsome, but good-natured, pleasant. Wayne is walking through a stand of loblolly pine with a pump spray can used to poison pine beetles. He looks sort of like an alien in the surgical mask and thick plastic goggles he wears to protect his lungs and eyes from the pesticide. Then out of a thicket comes Mr. Parker shouting in an almost foreign-sounding language. Wayne is just about to lower the mask to say hello when the old man pulls the trigger. The pleasant, not-quiet-handsome face is erased by a tight pattern of buckshot. The nose, the cheeks, the brow, everything is a bloody mess, everything but the eyes. The soft parts of the eyes are protected by the goggles.

The doctor gave Wayne's eyes to a little boy in Birmingham. Wayne had signed an organ donor card at college and hadn't bothered to tell anyone. The donation had upset Haze's parents, but it had given Wayne's wife, Loanne, a certain amount of comfort. Occasionally she talked to the little boy on the phone. Loanne was three months pregnant at Wayne's funeral. And now Mr. Parker was in a nursing home, blissfully unaware he'd ever done any harm.

Holding the gun gingerly, for a moment Haze pictured himself carelessly pulling the trigger and shattering the windows of the bedroom. He thought how horrible it would be if he lost his mind and went outside and shot his father in the face.

Wayne died about a month after Haze's birthday. Uncle

Poochie had given Haze the Remington as a present. Poochie was the Kennedy town constable and had all manner of firearms, both in his home and in the tiny office he occupied in the courthouse. The day Poochie had given Haze the rifle, they had gone on a crow hunt together. Haze liked to listen to his uncle Poochie talk about the places he'd been overseas in the military or about what the farm was like thirty or forty years ago when his grandfather farmed cotton on shares with a Negro family that had ten children.

"You know when I was your age there used to be gypsies around here," said Poochie as they stepped over the mill creek that separated Haze's daddy's property from his uncle's. "They'd come in wagons and ask for work. Only they didn't want to do anything hard like pick cotton. Gypsies always wanted to paint your barn or something." Poochie was a tall, thin man, not nearly as big or strong as Haze's daddy, but when he talked to Haze, Poochie looked him in the eye and not down his nose. "They buried a baby around here somewheres. One of their women was pregnant and ready to deliver, and so your Big Daddy told them that they could camp out here until it was born and the woman was ready to move. I think he half expected it was some sort of trick. But it wasn't. There was a miscarriage. They buried it in the woods around here and that was the last we ever saw of them. There are a few Indian graves around here, too."

"Indian graves?"

"Yeah buddy, before the government moved them out, this part of Alabama was Choctaw territory."

Haze thought about how the tiller would occasionally kick up an arrowhead out of the garden.

Poochie pulled a tiny cassette player out of his field jacket and pressed play. The tape inside began to screech and caw, and within moments a murder of crows spiraled above their heads. Poochie watched as Haze shouldered the Remington and fired toward the treetops. One crow fell dead through the branches, but the others flapped away before Haze could reload and get another shot.

Later, Poochie tied a strand of baling twine around the dead crow's feet and hung it up in a pecan tree next to his own house. "Look here, Haze," said Poochie, knotting the twine. "I know boys just want to go out and kill everything when they first get a gun, but you have to be careful. You can kill all the crows you want. They eat up everybody's corn and run off songbirds. Jays are mean as shit, too. You know what Big Daddy used to say about them?"

"No, what?"

"Every time he'd see a blue jay, he'd say, 'Jays go to hell on Friday.' So kill them, but don't let me catch you shooting songbirds—no bluebirds, or mockingbirds, or whooperwills. They're good luck and don't do anybody any harm. Okay?"

"Okay. How long you going to leave that crow hanging there?"

"As long as it takes his friends to figure out they ain't welcome here." Poochie reached back into his field jacket and handed Haze the cassette player. "Kill as many as you can."

Within a month Haze had hunted down over a dozen crows, and three or four of their oily, black-feathered corpses swung outside every window of the farm. It made Haze feel good to know he was protecting his family property, and it made him a little sad when the crows finally grew wise and refused to answer the call. By spring, Wayne was dead, and Haze's daddy wouldn't let Haze go hunting anymore. The crows returned. They bullied the bluebirds away from the yard and pecked kernels of Silver

Queen that Haze and his daddy had set out for roasting ears. Sometimes at night Haze would dream about Wayne's funeral. In the dream, the pallbearers would carry the heavy mahogany casket from the church to the cemetery, except someone had planted towering rows of Silver Queen among the headstones. On the edge of the first row of corn was an open, bottomless grave. Just before the pallbearers lowered Wayne's coffin into the pit, thousands of crows rushed out of the hole like bats out of a cave.

When Haze stepped out on the front porch with the rifle, he saw his daddy standing in the door of the old corncrib filing a hoe. He scraped the file across the flat edge of the blade until the dull steel took on a vicious, smiling gleam. Some years ago, when it became more convenient to buy feed corn from the grain elevator in Vernon, the crib was converted into a tool shed. Walking into the crib was like walking into a tiny museum of agriculture. Between the massive scaffolding of dirt dauber nests, the walls were decorated with four generations of tools: axes, crosscut saws, Kaiser blades, cricket plows, can hooks, obsolete tractor parts, and rotten leather mule skidders. Many of the tools, old and mysterious-looking, the boy couldn't even fathom their purpose.

By the time Haze had made it off the front porch, his father was walking back toward the barn. "Here." Haze's daddy offered the hoe handle to Haze and the boy took it. Haze's father extended his palm. "When I shoot him down, if he's still moving around you get him with this."

Haze held on to the gun. "Did you check on Loanne's kittens when you were in the crib?"

Haze's daddy looked up at the sky. "I don't have time to worry about any damn cats right now."

That morning at breakfast they had eaten only cold cereal because Haze's mother was going to drive Loanne to the doctor for a checkup. Everybody was surprised and grateful when Loanne decided to live on the farm and not move back in with her parents in Starkville. Haze's mother had tried to get her to move into the house with them, but Loanne said she liked living in Wayne's trailer while she attended nursing school.

Haze's mother had refilled her cereal bowl with milk and handed it to Haze. "Take this out to Whore Cat for me. I don't want her to go out hunting for something and leave her new kittens alone. Loanne's got her heart set on keeping those cats, and I don't want anything to happen to them."

"What does she want with kittens?" Haze had asked.

"Well, she says she wants to keep them in the Lonzo house to keep down on the mice." Wayne's trailer was only a few feet from the rundown house Haze's grandfather had built before the depression; they used the old house as a hay barn in the winter time. "But that's just an excuse. Don't you know she's lonely down there all by herself? I bet she brings one of them into the trailer with her by the time the baby's born." Haze's mother made a face. She didn't think much of living with cats or dogs in the house, but she was for anything that would make Loanne content.

Haze had carried the bowl of milk to the back porch, where the cats often slept curled up in peach baskets, but Whore Cat was nowhere to be found. Whore Cat was the oldest and wildest of the farm cats, and she had earned her name by constantly dropping litters under the Trulls' house. She was an ugly, skittish animal, an ill-patterned calico with pink wobbly teats that testified to her countless pregnancies, but she was a fierce hunter who lived off mice, lizards, and the leftover cornbread and pot likker the Trulls dumped in a hubcap next to the barn. Haze liked having the cats around the farm; the comings and goings of their quiet society made the place feel alive and slightly mysterious. The cats were always slithering in and out of the house's cinder-block foundation, conducting secret meetings behind the chimney and under the living-room floor.

Haze had eventually discovered the litter in the crib, lying on an oily T-shirt at the bottom of the ancient corn sheller. The corn sheller was a three-by-three cedar crate nailed to the wall like a trough. Attached to the right side of the cedar box was a crank that looked like an oversized sausage grinder. Before it was cost effective to buy feed grain by the truckload, a farmer would make a little at a time by feeding cobs of corn into the mouth of the crank and turning the handle. The teeth on the wheel inside gnawed off the kernels and left both the loose corn and the naked cob at the bottom of the crate.

Inside the empty crate, the kittens had been licked clean and looked like three glistening moles. What little fur they had was speckled yellow and orange, and he could see the pinkish gray flesh of their bellies expand and contract as they breathed. Whore Cat was gone, already on the prowl. She had moved the kittens into the crib for safekeeping, only Haze didn't think the crib was all that safe. Owls sometimes roosted in the rafters during the day. Thinking of Loanne, Haze had covered the corn sheller with a stray piece of roofing tin. Pushing the tin flush to the crank, he promised himself he would keep an eye out for Whore Cat's return so he could let her in to nurse. He left the bowl of milk on top of the tin, and then promptly forgot about the kittens until he saw his father sharpening the hoe in the doorway.

"Let me have the gun." Haze's father made a come-hither motion with his hand.

"Can I try and hit it?"

"No, you best let me do this. I don't want you cracking one of my birdhouses open."

My birdhouses. Haze's daddy made out like the whole farm belonged to him. "Come on, Daddy, please?"

Haze's daddy rolled his eyes. "I am too tired and in too much of a hurry to argue with you. All I know is if you miss, I'm going to take that gun away from you for good."

Haze blinked slowly and finally exchanged the rifle for the hoe. Just then Poochie's patrol car pulled into the drive, slinging gravel. The car door slammed. "Yo, Floyd!"

"Over here on the back side, Pooch!" Haze and his daddy waited a moment as Poochie made his way around the barn. Haze was surprised to see him still in his uniform.

"Where you been, Pooch? The sky's going to open up on us in an hour or so."

Haze's uncle held up his hand. "Hold up. Lois called me about an hour ago. There was a wreck after Loanne and her left the hospital. Lois is okay, but they're having to operate on Loanne. You better get over there as quick as you can."

Haze's daddy looked at Haze, and then at the hay field. "Is it serious? I mean, the baby?"

Haze's first thought was that somehow the wreck had damaged the baby's eyes, and wasn't it a shame that they had already given Wayne's eyes away to that boy in Birmingham. Then he could see by the expression on his uncle's face that it was more serious than that, and he thought about the dead gypsy baby's lost grave in the bottoms of the mill creek.

"Look, Loanne's momma and daddy are already driving to the hospital. You better get over there too."

By then Haze's daddy looked pale and dizzy. His hooded eyes

were bruised and puffy, as if the whole day had just been one punch in the face after another.

"What's with the rifle?"

Haze's daddy frowned and straightened. He pointed to the martin gourds where the exhausted birds were losing control of their circle. "Look up yonder, Pooch."

Poochie's sharp eyes spotted the snake immediately. "God almighty."

"I have to get it down before we can go." Haze's daddy shouldered the rifle and squinted. The rifle was too small for him, and Haze thought his father looked like an overgrown kid who had refused to give up a toy.

"You want my pistol?" Poochie unlatched the safety strap on his holster.

Haze's daddy shook his head and there was a small ping from the Remington. The martins scattered. The snake jerked its head back into the gourd, leaving only about an inch of its belly poking out of the opening. "I hit it." Haze's daddy's face grew angry. "I just didn't kill it."

Haze wanted to say something smart like, *Boy—I sure hope you don't crack one of my birdhouses*, but knew better.

"There's still a little of him sticking out, Floyd. You want me to take a shot?" Haze's daddy shook his head, shouldered the rifle, and fired. Grazed again, this time the snake had had enough. In an instant it tumbled out of the birdhouse and unraveled itself in the air. Time stood still as the three of them marveled at it—the flying snake—four feet of airborne serpent sailing toward them. Haze was shocked when the snake landed inches away from his boots and began to crawl. The boy had forgotten all about the hoe in his hands.

"Kill it, son," yelled Haze's daddy.

Haze hopped two steps and struck at the snake's head. The hoe blade missed and the snake veered. By the time Haze had the handle up in the air again, the snake was past him, headed for the barn. If the snake got under the barn, it would get away for sure. It managed to get its head into the tall johnsongrass next to the barn's corner when Poochie materialized, grabbed the snake by the tail, and lifted it up in the air. Constricting the massive muscles in its body, the chickensnake curled upward and bit deep into Poochie's hand. Poochie cursed and flung the snake away.

The snake hit Haze's daddy square in the chest, and Haze was stunned to hear his father scream. The boy was tempted to laugh, but realized if he did, he might scream too. But Haze's daddy quickly stamped his foot down on the middle of the twisting snake's black-and-yellow body. The snake reared its head and opened its jaws to reveal a glistening pink mouth. It struck, first at Haze's daddy's steel-tipped boots and then at his denim-covered leg. "Come here and kill this damn thing!"

Haze rushed toward his father, holding the hoe like a spear. First he knocked the snake away from his father's leg with the flat of the blade and then with a swift hack he beheaded the creature as easily as chopping the head off a milk thistle or morning glory. The headless snake became electric, a self-knotting rope that tangled and untangled itself, spinning around and around in the shorn pasture.

"Damn things are nothing but nerves," said Poochie holding his hand, blood dripping through his fingers. "See that yellow belly? Chickensnake for sure."

"Give me that." Haze's daddy reached for the hoe. He pressed the flat of the blade down on the writhing snake until the corpse was relatively still. Then he reached down and picked up the open tube of snake and began squeezing and massaging it with both hands. A yellow beak emerged, and then the whole head of a martin fledgling, its purple downy feathers slick with chyme. It looked as if it could have been one of the snake's own young. The fledgling fell to the ground near the snake's severed head, then another and another.

"Three little bitties," said Poochie wistfully.

"I could feel them under my foot when I stepped on him." Still holding the snake in both hands, Haze's father began to weep, just for a moment. He offered the dead snake to Haze.

Haze took it, felt the dry scales slide around the reptile meat as he closed his hands around it. "What do you want me to do?"

"Nail it up on the barn, high, somewhere the cats can't get to it. That'll keep any more of the bastards from taking up around here."

"What about the hay?"

Haze's daddy shrugged his shoulders. The black storm clouds had closed in, as if the sun had decided to set early. "Let it get rained on, I guess. Hell, let it come a flood. That's all I know to do."

Haze nodded, walked his father and uncle to the patrol car, and even opened the door for his father. When his daddy slumped into the passenger's side, Haze had never seen his old man look more defeated, not even at Wayne's funeral. Poochie hit the siren when they made it to the highway, and it gave Haze a quiet sense of relief. Finally he had a moment to himself.

Haze wondered if he could get the last load of hay off the truck before the rain hit. First he'd nail up the snake and then he'd at least try to get the hay into one of the mule stalls. Haze opened the crib door to look for a hammer when he was hit with the stench of spoiled milk. Whore Cat was standing on top of the corn sheller, and she had knocked the plastic cereal bowl Haze had left for her on the floor. The cat was mad and bleeding from a fight, maybe with another cat. Her right eye was filling up with pus. She hissed at Haze when he stepped into the doorway.

"Oh, God, cat, what have you been into?" Then Haze remembered the dead chickensnake he was holding in his hand. Haze dropped the snake outside the door so it wouldn't make the cat nervous. He continued to speak to Whore Cat in a hushed voice, and the more he talked the more she seemed to recognize him. She began mewling, making it clear she wanted to get to the kittens and nurse—*who was fool enough to put this tin between me and my brood?*

Haze picked up the cat and cradled her gently in his left arm, being careful not to hurt her swollen teats, which were damp with blood. Then Haze flipped off the tin with his right hand. He was just getting ready to place the mother cat in with her kittens when Whore Cat screamed and bit him, sinking her teeth into the flesh between his thumb and forefinger. Haze dropped her to the floor. The kittens were no longer asleep on the oily T-shirt. In their place lay the chickensnake's mate, curled up on the kittens' bed. The sallow yellow swirls along its body were grossly distended. After such a large meal, the snake was logy and could barely find the energy to open her eyes.

Haze stood there for what seemed like a long time before he puzzled it out, how the snake must have crawled through the corn sheller's crank, dropped down on the blind kittens, and smothered them in their sleep. After she swallowed them, she had swollen too fat to crawl past the crank's teeth. Haze had set a perfect snake trap and used the kittens for bait.

Haze picked up a stray ax handle, but he couldn't bring himself to crush the chickensnake's head. What was he going to tell Loanne? What was he going to do with the snake after he killed it—nail it up on the barn with the kittens still inside? He didn't have the stomach to cut them out. For the first time since Wayne's funeral Haze was alone on the vast farm, and he didn't know what to do. Behind him, Haze heard more mewling. He turned. The dead chickensnake outside had drawn the attention of five or six cats from the barn. The big tawny tom was licking blood from the open neck of the corpse. The tom looked up at Haze with blood on its nose, as if to say, *Get used to it*. Then he clamped down on the snake with his jaws, dragging the headless body backward under the crib.

That's when it started to rain. The remaining cats scattered for cover. Heavy drops beat down on the crib, reminding Haze of the tin roof over his own head. Like the snake in the corn sheller, he felt trapped. He balled up his fist, squeezing blood out of the deep cat bite. Cats have filthy mouths, his mother would say if she were here—infection, rabies, cat scratch fever. She would have ordered him to wash his hands and treat the wound with peroxide on the spot. He stared out of the crib as the rain began to soak the hay.

Eventually he found the strength to turn from the door and lift the ax handle. Inching toward the sheller, he peered over into the corn trough and poised the handle just over the sleepy snake's head. Reluctantly, the swollen snake began to uncoil, the newborn kittens weighing it down like tumors. For a moment, Haze felt a pang of sympathy for the snake in a way he knew his father never would have. No real farmer wasted sympathy on snakes. But after all, it was only a snake, doing what snakes do. Haze felt sorry for it almost as much as he felt sorry for himself. Crushing the snake's head wouldn't change the fact that Whore Cat's kittens were dead, nor the martin fledglings neither. No matter how many snakes he crushed or crows he shot, he just couldn't stop the world from eating itself.

Mule

Owen O'Shields pulled his pickup into the teachers' parking lot of Lurleen Wallace High School out of habit. Only after he killed the motor did he remember he no longer worked there. For a moment he considered moving to the general parking lot in the back where people parked for ballgames, but the school day was over and most of the teachers had already gone home; he wasn't taking up needed space. He stepped out of his truck and pulled his baseball cap down over his ears. It was raining. Alongside the wide awning that covered the school's front doors, two yellow buses, 78 and 112, now on their second routes, had stopped just long enough to load the last students bound for home. The buses' windshield wipers bounced back and forth, as regular as metronomes. Owen knew the women who captained these bright-yellow mammoths; they were teachers picking up extra money, both of them near retirement age. He raised his hand in a wave as he ducked under the awning, water trailing down the aluminum overhead. Safe from the rain, he took off his cap and entered the dimly lit corridor. The school buses rolled away even before the steel doors shut behind him, and the rumble of the departing engines detonated a strong surge of nostalgia that left him woozy.

On unsure legs, Owen walked down the sloping hallway toward the auditorium, where the cheerleaders assembled in the afternoons. When he reached the entrance, he quietly peered inside. Immediately he spied Amber, his stepdaughter, standing at the base of a human pyramid of lovely teenagers. Owen was glad his stepdaughter, tall and statuesque like her mother, was not one of those ninety-eight-pound pixie girls the male cheerleaders flung up in the air like rag dolls, looking up their skirts every chance they got. He had married two years ago after a lifetime of bachelorhood, but it hadn't taken Owen long to learn to play the part of the worried father. Amber was attractive and outgoing, and when he'd worked at the school, he had seen for himself that the boys followed her around the hallways like a pack of love-addled hounds. Owen entered the auditorium and leaned against the wall, hoping to observe his new daughter tumble and cheer awhile before he reached his final destination, the maintenance office.

When the pyramid disassembled there was a great deal of squealing and clapping. In the midst of the jangle, Amber caught sight of Owen and, without the least concern for what others might think, ran toward him full-speed, tackling him with a hug that made him flush with both love and fear. Why was he afraid? Maybe it was because he could feel the ample weight of his stepdaughter's breasts pressing into his chest and it embarrassed him that he noticed. Maybe he was just afraid that soon the hug would have to end. He had never been a father before, and it seemed sad that soon Amber would be grown and married, gone away before he got a chance to really be her daddy. Owen patted Amber gently on the back and looked up to see the girls' coach frowning in their direction. Owen gave her a sheepish wave. Until his retirement a few short months ago, Owen had been one of the vice principals of Lurleen Wallace High. Having once been her boss, it annoyed him that the girls' coach felt free to frown at him openly.

"What are you doing here?" Amber asked, untangling her limbs from his.

"Oh, I came to see Mr. Amos. I loaned him some tools I need to get back. I thought I'd come and look in on y'all's practice before I hunted him down."

"Did the stud come today?"

Owen felt a tic of jealousy move through his body. He hoped it had not registered on his face. "Oh, yeah. He's there, running around like he owns the place."

The new horse had arrived at the stables only a few hours before. The stud was solid black, stood sixteen hands high, and weighed just over half a ton. His chest was broad and smooth like a bar of iron a blacksmith had beaten to flat perfection; his long, muscular legs dovetailed into his haunches like the work of a master carpenter. The horse's arrogant, marbled head, a model of equine conformation, looked as if it belonged atop the dark square of a chess set. Within the aquiline skull, behind the long, fine lashes, the stud's roving eyes fixed upon everything around him, whether living or dead, with a suspicion that bordered on hate. When he looked at Owen, Owen could feel the hate radiating off the brute like heat from a stove eye.

"I can't wait to see him. I'll bet he's beautiful. Just beautiful."

"He's something, all right," said Owen, gently pushing her away. "You better fall back in formation or Coach Simmons will make us both run laps."

Amber gave Owen a grin that lit up her freckles. Then quick as a minnow, she darted back into the school of teenagers with their deep-blue-and-white uniforms. Owen watched them tumble and clap as he walked the perimeter of the auditorium. Just before exiting, he witnessed Amber boost a tiny redheaded girl up on her solid shoulders. The redhead held her left hand up to her eyes like a visor, as if she were in the process of observing some brave new landscape and had discovered there, "Wildcats! Wildcats! Go Wildcats! Yeaaaa!"

Wildcat, he thought, maybe that would be the name Amber would choose to give the stud. Amber named all the animals on the farm: the horses, the heifers, the cats, the dogs, the hutch of goslings Owen had given her for Christmas. Amber spent many long hours picking out the perfect name for each critter. She even bought a book of baby names to help her with the process. But whatever they ended up calling the stud, Owen knew the horse's real name was Trouble.

Upon arrival, the stud had backed out of the trailer kicking at the steel doors so violently that there was concern he might injure himself. Sue, Amber's mother, decided not to put him in a stall or even the corral until he had a chance to calm down. She turned him loose in the small green pasture behind the stables, where the stallion ran full-speed through the misting rain toward one edge of the barbed-wire fence, only to stop inches away from the line, spin about like a dancer, kicking sheets of rainwater off the fescue under his hooves, and then race toward the opposite stretch of wire.

"Let him run the evil out of himself," Sue said, taking off her Stetson-style patrolman's hat and shaking the water off the plastic rain guard. She adjusted her tight blond braid. This was how she dressed for work when she went on ride-alongs with the Tuscaloosa County Sheriff's Department. She had on her brown-and-yellow slicker, too, with the five-point star on the breast. "When he's good and tired we can get a fresh start."

"How long you reckon that's going to be?" asked Owen. He took his glasses off and cleaned the vapor condensing on the lenses with the blue bandana he kept in the hip pocket of his jeans.

"I don't know. A horse built like him, could be a long time," said Sue smiling, clearly as pleased with herself as she was with the stud.

Owen watched as the stud ran along the entire perimeter of the fence. Each time the horse's running room evaporated, he whinnied and screamed as if part of the world had been snatched away from him.

"I still don't know why you'd want to buy a horse like that. He's heartbreak waiting to happen."

"He's goddamn gorgeous is what he is, Double O. The stud fees alone will pay for him in a couple years. Besides, I've told you, Amber wants a foal out of Mix to help raise this summer, and I aim to give her one. She's had Mix her whole life. Her daddy gave her that horse when she was ten and pretty soon she's going to be too old to breed. Besides, it'll give Amber something more constructive to do than lay out at the lake and talk on her cell phone all summer." Sue shoved her fists into the pockets of her jacket as if to say *There, period, end of conversation.*

They had been having this argument ever since Sue had spotted the stud in the online version of the Quarter Horse Trader. Around Christmas Sue had started talking about early retirement from her job as a psychologist with social services. Now that Owen's pension checks were coming in every month, she thought they had the resources they needed to turn the stables into a real horse farm, to start training, breeding, and giving lessons full-time. But to have a real horse farm, Sue thought she had to have a badass in the stables. Owen had told her he was all in favor of her retiring. His nerves were frayed from his last few years of teaching, and he worried when she was out in the field. But what was the point of trading one dangerous job for another?

Seeing the stud wheel about the pasture, Owen said, "He's vicious as all hell, Sue. It'll be like boarding a death-row convict."

"He's three, Double O, and high-strung. He'll calm down soon enough." She took her right hand out of her slicker and made a motion as if she were shooing a fly.

Owen knew he should let it drop but couldn't. "Well, I'm not sure I'd want my daughter messing around with anything as hellacious as what's liable to come out of that son of a bitch."

Sue went cross-eyed. "Yeah, well, she's not your daughter. So let me worry about that." Sue winced as soon as she said it, but she then set her jaw, refusing to let regret take hold of her.

Owen managed to put his glasses on and turn away from her in one fluid motion. "All right, she's your daughter. He's your horse," Owen said over his shoulder. "But when he tears this place down around y'all's heads don't blame me. Stand out here like a turkey in the rain and marvel all you want; I'm heading for the house." Owen tromped off, leaving Sue to unhitch the gooseneck trailer and the brake lights from the ton truck by herself.

As soon as Owen stepped out of the auditorium, cold rain slapped him in the face, and the memory of Sue's barb angered and frustrated him. The sky was almost black now. Outside he looked across the student parking lot toward the field house; beyond it the football coach was making the team duck-walk around the goalpost. On a rainy day like today, Owen hoped the bastard would have sense enough to bring them in soon. Most of the team would still be worn and frayed from August's relentless two-a-day practices. He knew that a winning team had to be tough, but the coach was a silly son of a bitch who literally didn't have enough sense to come in out of the rain. "Another turkey," Owen said to himself out loud. "He'll give the whole team pneumonia." Owen disliked the coach. He was a belligerent, fat man whose manner had often forced Owen to counsel with outraged parents. The coach's contract also stipulated that he got full teaching wages in the summer for simply cutting the grass. The school could barely pay for toilet paper, and the fat bastard made more than Owen had just for riding around on a John Deere on Friday afternoons.

The maintenance shed was connected to the field house where Mr. Amos, the head custodian, kept his office. But Owen knew Mr. Amos would be busy now, directing his clean-up crew. Owen walked across the parking lot and entered the other side of the building, stepping into a row of empty classrooms. The hallways echoed with his footsteps. This building was as familiar to him empty as it was full of students; it was a lonely thing, a school without children.

The last three years of his career had been the worst. He'd quit teaching social studies and had accepted a position as one of the vice principals in order to up the payout of his retirement checks. Being in administration meant he'd lost his summers off. He was used to breaking a sweat in the hot months and not sitting meekly in the air-conditioned office playing phone tag with wheedling textbook reps and running defense for the principal when relations with the superintendent were strained.

Owen would have much rather been out in the open field on his blue Ford tractor, clearing brush with his Bush Hog and cutting hay with the mower. His father had died the same year he had become vice principal, so Owen had sold the old man's last few head of cattle that had grazed clean the old cotton fields of his youth. He then contracted with Weyhauser to set the open pasture out in pine to go alongside the 120 acres of hardwood that kept the farm hidden from highway traffic. Soon after, he began the thuggish business of running a school: checking lockers, dispensing licks with a thick wooden paddle, and meeting with irate parents that often as not would threaten to whip his ass right in front of their child. Nothing about the job, other than the money, was satisfying. Those last three years, he learned the names of only the worst students, those troubled young creatures, most of them drugged and abused, who paced back and forth through the halls like angry zoo animals, dreaming of the day they'd grow old enough to drop out. Only Sue had kept him together in the first year, still battling the grief over his father. Sue always encouraged him, telling him how important his job was—he saved lives, she said.

"No, that's what you do. I just keep them pieced together with bubble gum and pipe cleaners from eight in the morning 'til three-fifteen in the afternoon and hope they make it back alive the next day." Even then he knew, strictly speaking, this wasn't true. He had broken up knife fights, performed CPR on a basketball player with an undiagnosed heart condition, even saved a whole bus full of kids once when he'd spotted torn tread on the right back tire. But mostly he watched them, watched them the way a sheepdog watches a herd, silent and serious. Rarely a day went by when he didn't spot the germ of some hidden danger waiting to blossom.

But Sue was the real lifesaver. She worked in tandem with social services, the sheriff's department, and the county schools. When there was a report of child abuse, Sue was the investigator who decided whether the kid should be removed from the home immediately or undergo further observation. When a child was removed from the home by force, Sue was there to comfort the stunned boy or girl about to be delivered into foster care and, if possible, to reason with the parents almost always threatening violence. If she couldn't reason with them, she would help arrest them. Though her salary was funded by social services, she had trained in the police academy in Tuscaloosa and had been deputized. She kept a badge in her wallet, a Kevlar vest in the extended cab of her Toyota Tacoma, and a nine-millimeter Glock in the glove compartment.

After the removal of an older child from an abusive home, Sue would visit Owen's office in order to apprise the school of any potential problems. After his first meeting with Sue Bonny, Owen had done some asking around about her and discovered she was Spencer Bonny's widow, the fire captain who had died of a heart attack a few years back at the West Alabama Fair Grounds. When Sue made her follow-up report concerning a father molesting one of the girls in Mrs. Upright's homeroom, Owen enticed her out on a lunch date with the promise of selling her the hay in his father's barn for cheap. The talk turned from hay to the price of feed, then to people they knew in common at the co-op, then to the other farmers who lived in Tuscaloosa County, what they raised and how they treated their kids.

After Sue had hurt Owen's feelings earlier that afternoon, he had trudged off around the corral, then paused briefly at the mound of pine chips he'd recently purchased to line the stalls. Damn, why hadn't he put a tarp on them this morning before it started to drizzle? Owen hurried toward the stables, relieved to be out of the wet air. Mix, Amber's blood bay mare, stuck her nose out of the stall and peered out intently. Owen had forgotten to give her her oats. Since Amber had cheerleading practice in the afternoons, Owen would have to feed the horses and muck out the stalls until football season was over. Annoyed, Owen walked past Mix. As he came close, Mix retreated back into the darkness of her stall, as did Sue's gelding, Desoto. Unlike the stud, these were friendly creatures who should have been made more friendly by hunger. They could probably tell just by the seismic quality of Owen's footsteps that Owen was pissed. Everything people said about horses being sensitive was true. No matter what their individual demeanors, horses didn't do well around intense feelings. Even pure joy could send them into a quivering panic. God made the horse an emotional barometer.

Owen made his way to the middle of the stables and unhooked the chain to the feed room. The tarp was high on the top shelf with various vitamins, powders, and food supplements, all of them advertising essential amino acids or glossy coats. The plywood shelf stretched out like a mantel over the ancient Frigidaire deep freeze, dead now twenty years, but still a good, airtight place to keep feed from going stale. On each side of the freezer there were stacks of empty Ripsnorter sweet-feed sacks. Owen reached up on top of the shelf for the folded tarp and tucked it under his arm, exited the feed room, and made his way back down the long corridor to the end of the stables. His jaw clenched as he braced for the unpleasant pin drops of rain that pelted his face like birdshot. By the time he covered the pine chips, his baseball cap was wet and his glasses had fogged up again.

Already he was replaying the argument in his head. He did not expect Sue to run after him, nor did he expect that she would find a quiet moment in the evening or the next day to apologize. He had realized only after they had married that Sue never apologized for anything. If he acted hurt, she would resent the fact she'd hurt him and hold that against him too. *Not your daughter*— damn, what an ugly thing to say. He loved Amber, loved her as much as Sue would let him. Sometimes it seemed like Sue tried to keep them distant.

Once when Amber and Sue had returned from an all-day trail ride, Amber had tutored Owen in the proper way to way to bathe a horse. "You can't turn the hose on one like a dog. You'll scare the fool out of her. You have to distract her. You have to sing to her."

"Sing?" Owen pointed at the five-gallon pail full of warm water and laundry detergent at Amber's feet. "I couldn't carry a tune in that bucket right there."

"It don't matter what you sing or how you sing it. The important thing is you take the horse's mind off the fact you are fooling with her. Give her a tune to pay attention to so she's not always looking for boogers in the shadows."

"That's easy for you to say. You're in the choir. Didn't your friend Carmen ask you to sing at her wedding?"

"Harmon," Amber corrected. "Here I'll sing with you."

And so they sang the only song Owen knew all the words to, "Amazing Grace." With a wavering but happy harmony, they soaped and lathered the perplexed horse. For an encore they sang the first verse of "If Heaven Ain't a Lot Like Dixie" as Amber held Mix's halter and Owen hosed her off like a car.

"We had a good time washing Mix today, didn't we, Daddy-O?" Amber announced at dinner later that night. She balled up her fist and kneaded it into Owen's upper arm. Despite a volley of good-natured tomboy punches, Owen managed to serve his plate. *Daddy-O*; it had all the makings of a fine nickname, something more intimate than *Mr. O'Shields,* something less awkward than *Owen*, but Sue didn't react well to the *Daddy* and the *O* getting mixed up together, and she gave the girl a withering look that wilted the salad and turned the hamburger steak grease-cold.

Still, Owen was just starting to feel like the three of them belonged together. *Not your daughter*—hadn't Sue realized how low saying something like that would make him feel? Why hadn't he snapped back, *Well then, why am I paying for your daughter to go to college next year?* But Owen had never been that quick on his feet, had he? It angered him that he could only think of the right things to say long after the right time to say them had passed. *Not your daughter, not your daughter*—the words reverberated in the cavelike hollows of his imagination. Sometimes it was hard to believe that Sue was a psychologist. Or maybe it wasn't, maybe she knew exactly how low saying something like that would make him feel.

Damn, he was daydreaming in the rain. Owen unfolded the

tarp like a bedsheet and covered the mushy chips, saving them from further saturation. Then he trotted back to the safety of the stables. He stood for a moment in the mouth of the wide double doors and cleaned his glasses again. Because of the corral, he could see neither Sue nor the stud, so he simply watched the rain grow heavy as he rubbed the bandana in soft circles around his bifocals.

Sue's first husband, Spencer, would have probably slapped her face for her if she had ever talked to him so ugly. Owen had taught Spencer seventh grade world history thirty years ago, Owen's very first class. Spencer Bonny—he'd been third on the roll, right behind Anders and Askew. Spencer had been a hellion even then, unruly and wild as a cartoon cowboy. Once he'd brought a cap gun to school in his lunch box and held up the lunchroom lady that took up dollars for hot lunches and milk. That was back in the day before you suspended kids for things like that. Back then you just beat the hell out of them with a thick piece of wood and set them to washing the school's windows or helping Mr. Amos pick up trash after the final bell.

Still Spencer couldn't have been all bad. He'd built this place with his own two hands: the house, the barn, the corral, the stables—the carpentry was first rate, not so much as one jagged splinter hanging off the lumber to mar the workmanship, not so much as one loose piece of tin atop the stables to disrupt the even tone of the rain beating down over his head. Owen looked up at the high rafters where the wood and tin joined. Faintly he heard mewling over his head, tiny cries echoing off the underbelly of the roof. High in the honeycomb of the hay, the cats that lived in the loft were hungry, too.

Owen again walked past Mix and Desoto, past the tack and dressing area, back to the feed room. He opened the lid of the old deep freeze. Using a Red Diamond coffee can as a measuring cup, Owen scooped out a level quart of sweet feed and another of oats and deposited them in one of the empty gallon ice cream buckets at the bottom of the freezer. The rich smell of industrial molasses wafted up into the damp air, as if a cloud of syrup were just about to accumulate overhead.

Desoto, as always, knocked Owen out of the way to get his feed. But Mix waited for Owen to leave before she would lower her muzzle into the trough. She was a shy creature, and Owen cringed at the thought of the rough way the stud would come after the mare when Sue had her bred. They would probably tie her to a tree at the edge of the pasture or even shank her in the dressing room and allow the brute to rape her there. In a strange way, Mix's refusal to eat with him in the stall made Owen feel worse, like a lonely Adam exiled from the garden; even the beasts of the field had withdrawn fellowship. "Good ole Spence was a real horseman through and through," Sue had told Owen on more than one occasion, and Owen couldn't help but to feel that in some subtle way he was being unfavorably compared. Spencer had died with his spurs on, so to speak, a massive heart attack during the barrel races at the West Alabama Horse Show. His stallion had dragged his limp body round and round the sandy rink of the PARA fairgrounds until one of the line judges could catch the quarter horse and unhook the dead man's boot from the stirrup. Rumor had it he was drunk. Still Spencer had made it through school, made a fire captain out of himself and was insured to the gills—he'd left enough to pay for most of the land and the property. The new stud was probably the son of a bitch's reincarnation come back to claim everything he'd purchased in death.

Owen fed the boarded horses on the other side of the stables.

Two gaited paints, a purebred Arabian, and a pathetic little Shetland pony, fat, old, practically oozing glue. A rich doctor had bought the pony for his little girl, and they came to ride it about twice a year. Still, the checks for the boarding fees came on time. The other three belonged to deputies who worked with Sue. Most of the cops were hunters who contented themselves with expensive rifles and four-wheelers. Those who fished bought boats. The few that remained bought horses they couldn't afford. The checks for their boarding fees floated in haphazardly, if at all. Nothing Owen's pension couldn't absorb, but he resented having to foot the bill for them. Owen guessed he should be grateful, as the horses' owners looked out after Sue. He was afraid to complain—if he did, and something bad happened to her, well, he'd never forgive himself, would he?

It was growing dark in the stables. Owen flipped the light switch near the back doors that electrified the barn. The raw light bulb dangling over the dressing area in the middle of the stables came alive, and the old hi-fi system in the saddle room flooded the hall with music. The music kept the horses calm, and for this reason the dial never wavered from the country oldies station, not that Owen would have had it any other way. Smooth crooners like Willie Nelson and George Jones worked wonders on the horses' nerves. You couldn't tune in to any of that new Nashville crap with all the drums and synthesizers. You might as well light a string of Black Cat firecrackers and toss it under the horses' hooves. Owen turned over a plastic five-gallon bucket, sat down, and listened to Bobbie Gentry sing "Ode to Billie Joe."

The song took him back to his childhood. He had been raised on a cotton farm, where he plowed and chopped his way through the late 1940s and much of the fifties until the boll weevils ruined everything. Though he knew relatively little of horses, Owen knew everything there was to know about mules. Often as an adult, trapped in the air-conditioned nightmare of his office, he had wished for a pair of mules and forty acres of terraced topsoil to plow. Strangely enough, mules had more horse sense than horses and were usually less stubborn, certainly less flighty. You didn't have to serenade a mule to make him stand still. A mule understood both the carrot and the stick and between the two you could form a more-or-less permanent relationship. A mule could be mean as hell, for sure, but once you established a working contract with them, it seldom changed. A certain amount of trust developed. With Sue and her horses, things were always up for renegotiation. One minute you could be rubbing Soto's nose and the next, if you weren't careful, your hand would be in his mouth.

When Owen was a teenager, he had watched as his fifteen-year-old cousin Sarah, a voluptuous brunette, had her breast bitten off by his father's mare, Sugar, a loveable old nag named for her sweet disposition. Sarah and her parents had come to visit after church one Sunday, and after dinner Sarah and Owen gathered up green apples to feed the graying old mare. They fed Sugar apple after apple, until a sour green froth coated the fine gray whiskers on her muzzle and chin. Holding the very last apple, Sarah extended her hand to the horse's lips, forgetting to hold her hand flat the way Owen had shown her. Sugar nosed the apple to the ground, then playfully darted her nose up under Sarah's arm and clamped down onto her left breast. There was a scream and Owen was surprised to discover it was coming from him. The rest was a strange mix of blood, ripping cloth and soft tissue. Almost like a silent movie, Owen remembered Sarah gripping her chest as if in the throes of a heart attack. Terrified, the horse stood back on her heels and trembled, the sour green froth on her mouth now pink with blood, the very sheen of a perfect and healthy lung.

Owen sat through two more sets of oldies before he had finished formulating his plan. When he finally rose, he closed the double doors at the back entrance and said, "Good-bye, Mix. Good-bye, Soto. I got to see a man about a mule."

"Mr. O'Shields?"

Owen turned from the window from which he had been staring. Behind him stood Mr. Amos, the maintenance man, shouldering a hundred-foot-long extension cord. His navy blue coveralls, adorned with grease, seemed to shimmer around his dark flesh.

"Hey there, Mr. Amos."

"Why, Mr. O., it's good to see you." Mr. Amos was one of those ageless black men who could be anywhere from sixty to a hundred. He had tiny, almost gritty-looking creases around his eyes, as if his sockets needed to be recaulked. When the janitor extended his hand, Owen noticed the flesh on his palms looked like shrimp. He had not shaken the man's hand in almost thirty years, not since the day Owen was hired as a history teacher.

"I would've allowed you'd seen enough of this place."

"Maybe I have." Owen careened his neck around wistfully. "But I came to see you."

"Did you now?"

Later, in the maintenance office, Mr. Amos offered Owen one of the two padded folding chairs next to his desk. "Would you like a drink?"

Before Owen could even form a disapproving expression, the old man had unlocked the bottom drawer to his big steel green desk, World War II army surplus no doubt, and set a bottle of Thunderbird upon the flat surface which, other than the bottle, contained only an old rotary phone and a framed picture of Mr. Amos's ten grown children. Mr. Amos's drinking was the only case of alcoholism at Lurleen Wallace that every school administrator, including Owen, willfully ignored. It was easy to ignore, for it was as invisible as Mr. Amos himself.

"Sure. What the hell." Owen grinned. "What are they going to do, fire me?"

Mr. Amos selected a conical paper cup from the water cooler and filled it with a shot of cheap wine. Mr. Amos did not seem to drink because he was depressed or angry. In fact, Mr. Amos was the only employee of the school that never had a dark word concerning the state proration of funds that had prevented any of them from getting a raise in the last five years. Of all the people Owen had worked with on a daily basis, Mr. Amos was the only one whom Owen actually liked.

"I was wondering if you might like to go in on a little business venture with me."

Both Owen and Mr. Amos threw back a swallow of the cheap wine. Afterward Mr. Amos shrugged. "What did you have in mind?"

"I got a hundred and fifty acres in hardwood up on my daddy's old place, but I don't want it clear cut. I want the big trees skidded out. I want somebody to help me that knows how to reason with mules. You're one of the only fellows left I know of that's familiar with that kind of work atall."

Mr. Amos looked thoughtfully upward toward the ceiling. Owen choked down his wine and made a face. Before he knew it, Mr. Amos had topped off Owen's Dixie cup. "I haven't fooled with mules for a coon's age," said Mr. Amos. "Not since I took this job here. Last one we owned was called Chicken."

"Chicken? Why'd you call him that?"

"It was a jenny. She was bad to eat chickens. She had a solid black nose and they say that will make one mean as possum fuck. Any chicken that managed to toddle into her stall got its head bit off."

"Yeah, we had one that would do that very thing. We called him Frank." Owen took another sip of his wine, momentarily studying the tan imprint of vines and flowers running the length of the paper cup in his hand. "He even got holt of a half-grown cat one time and bit a chunk out of her back. He wouldn't let nobody plow him but my daddy. If one of us kids got behind him, he'd either run away with us or just lie down like he was sick. When I was thirteen, I quit dinner early one day and hooked him up to the singletrees by myself, then I got behind him and said, 'Step up,' and I slapped him across the neck with the reins. He laid his ears back and sulled up. I told him again, 'Step up, mule,' but he just stood there. I told him a third time, and when I did I laid my daddy's hickory walking stick across his skull. It took him by surprise all right. He fell to his knees, and I whacked him again hard enough that the shock made my fingers ache. When everybody came out of the house from dinner, me and Frank were laying down rows straight as a plumb line. After that me and Frank had no problems. We were pals."

Mr. Amos smiled at Owen's story, and then pointed at the picture of his family on his desk. "Too bad you can't do children that away."

"Or wives," said Owen.

For a moment, he felt proud to remember a time when he

just wasn't going to stomach feeling small and insignificant any-more. He was thirteen, damn it, and it was time for folks to listen to him, to recognize the fact that he carried weight and importance in the world, even if the first to make this realization was only Frank, a cranky and embittered chicken-killing mule. But breaking Frank had a ripple effect. From that day on Owen had an easier time looking people in the eye, his father and brothers spoke to him with less condescension in their voices, his mother served him coffee at breakfast.

"I never heard you tell that one, Mr. O.," said the janitor, topping off the Dixie cups once again.

"Mr. Amos, this is the first time I've thought of that story in thirty years. It's like remembering a dream. If you hadn't said anything about a mule killing chickens, it would be like it never happened."

"But it did," said the old man.

Owen took another sip from his Dixie cup. "Yeah, I guess it did at that." The two swapped mule stories for over an hour. When they were both good and drunk, they agreed to meet the next Saturday to drive up to a stockyard in Chattanooga that specialized in mules to select a span. They shook on it.

When Owen exited the building, he was surprised to find the stars were out. His truck sat alone in the empty parking lot. He couldn't go home like this. Then he remembered the hungry cats mewling around the hay and decided to sober up at the Wal-Mart. On a whim he invested in a chainsaw, a $600 Husqvarna with a twenty-inch nose bar and a Halloween-orange crankcase. The purchase made him feel like he'd made a commitment to the mule-skidding operation, that it wasn't all drunk talk. It felt like he was stepping into his own. For two years now Owen had been fixing Sue's fences and cutting her hay; he wouldn't have had it any other way. And yet, he wondered if he was doing much more than that. Okay, so she was independent, he knew that when he married her. But having an expensive, wild stud in the stables—she hadn't come up with that all on her own. That was Spencer's dream, and Owen wasn't sure how long he could live in another man's dream, especially one he found so dangerous.

Owen drove home slowly, his hands at the ten and two o'clock positions. The alcohol had been ebbing out of his bloodstream ever since he'd exited the school, and it left him with an ache behind his eyes. The white stripes in the median of the road were blurry, and they rose up to meet him faster than he expected. It made him feel nervous and out of control. Owen almost ran off the road when the sirens of an ambulance interrupted his concentration. At first he thought it was a police officer pulling him over. When he saw no blue lights in the rearview, he realized it must be an ambulance, but he still couldn't tell if the sound was in front of him or behind. Eventually the white and red lights appeared ahead on a hill in the distance. As it passed, he couldn't help but imagine Amber inside, her left breast lost in the black maw of the stud.

Owen gave a small prayer of thanks when he pulled into the drive. He got out of the truck and walked around the passenger's side of the door, hefting the fifty-pound bag of Special Kitty cat food up on his left shoulder and grabbing hold of the chainsaw with his right hand. Odd the lights were on in the barn and not in the house. By this time, Owen figured Sue and Amber would be watching TV in their bed clothes. As he tromped closer to the stables he heard singing, but it sounded funny, like maybe someone had finally turned the dial away from the old honky-tonk station to something classical. The notes were clear and articulated even though Owen couldn't understand the words.

By the time he made it to the entrance of the stables, Owen understood that the music wasn't coming from the radio but from Amber. She was singing "Ave Maria," the song she had sung at her friend Harmon's wedding. As Owen peered inside, he saw Amber and Sue standing on either side of the stud. The horse's ears drooped in a sleepy manner; his wet, languid body was still and calm as the women's hands stroked and caressed his neck with their curry combs. Owen listened intently outside the door to the glorious music, each note lodging into his heart. His entire life he had waited for a family that would love him for his slow and steady ways, and now he had come back home to find them worshiping at the foot of a dangerous idol. Owen's first impulse was to burst into the room and admonish them like an Old Testament prophet. But what good would that do? That would only drive them further away. The stud would have to hurt one of them for Sue to apologize to him now. In his mind he conjured up an image of the stud becoming spooked by a sudden shadow or noise, then rearing up and trampling both of them with his powerful hooves. Instead of music, Owen longed to hear his daughter scream. He ached to hear his wife wail with sorrow and regret. At that moment, it was only the mule in him that prevented him from pulling the cord on the chainsaw and announcing his presence with its gleaming, jealous teeth.

What Happens in the 'Burg, Stays in the 'Burg

This is a story about how loneliness and desperation can drive you to make the worst kind of decisions, the kind that, if you're lucky, won't destroy your life but will simply serve as a reminder of the pathetic weakness you are capable of, like the time you made it home safely after seven scotch and sodas at the office Christmas party only to crash your car into the garage door, or the time, in a fit of misplaced passion, you fumbled to kiss your best friend's wife in her kitchenette, where she gave you a sad, disappointed smile and shook her head slightly as you reached for her again, spilling a glass of shiraz on her blouse.

This is the story of how I came to fall in love with the wrong person, and though it ended in a minor disaster, as of yet I cannot bring myself to regret it, though soon I probably will. The setting? My subsidized faculty home in Russellville, Arkansas, on the edge of a small agricultural-university campus, a year ago, let's say, though of course the story began much earlier than that, and now that it is over, it still plays in a continuous loop, like celluloid film strung between the twin reels of my heart and mind.

The morning after my first soon-to-be-annual fish fry and croquet party, I woke feeling like a castaway, stranded on the desert island of my empty bed, dehydrated and panicky. I staggered to the bathroom for water and then lurched for the medicine cabinet over the sink. The doctor had given me a prescription for Lorazepam to help me with my recurrent anxiety attacks, but the medicine bottle contained only a tiny piece of paper that read, "Sorry—needed to come down. ☹" My grad students had evidently discovered my meds the night before and pilfered the contents. With such a mild tranquilizer, they had probably crushed all of it up and snorted it. The house was a mess. There were used paper plates and beer bottles on every surface, even the TV. The general disarray added to the pervasive stranger-in-a-strange-land feeling I had been experiencing ever since Gillian's departure a month before.

The party had been an attempt to cheer myself up, as I wouldn't be traveling to our friends' cabin on Rodanthe this year. It was a summer ritual we had practiced since before we were married; every July Gillian and I drove out to the North Carolina coast and stayed ten days or so with Mike Auden, my bud from grad school, and an assortment of our classmates from the University of Cincinnati. I had not been disinvited, technically. But

I had been asked to stay in a hotel a couple of miles away from the cabin. Mike's wife, Sheila, and Gillian were close, and I knew the kind of pressure a wife could put on a man to do something he didn't really want to do. So I didn't blame Mike, but I also knew that because I declined the invitation, I'd never get another. I didn't really understand what was going on, since Gillian and I had slept in the same bed until she moved out at the beginning of the summer. We'd sworn we would always be true friends and never create a situation where others would have to choose between us, but evidently something had changed since her return to Ohio.

"Everybody still wants you to come," Gillian had said to me when I called her in a rage of whys and how comes. She spoke sweetly, as if an unmelted pat of butter rested squarely on her tongue. I could hear sirens in the background, a sound that brought goose pimples to the back of my neck. We'd lived on Ludlow Avenue just a mile or so from campus, and Gillian had returned to our old apartment complex there. Within a mile of it, there were eight hospitals, a police station, and a firehouse; the street was in a constant state of emergency. Gillian thought Arkansas too quiet, I guess. We were both native southerners, but she had become an urbanite during our years in the city, while I had yearned for the slow, calm pace of home.

"No one wants to exclude you, Ian."

"A hotel. Jesus, Gil. I was visiting Mike at the cabin before I even met you."

"I'll say it again. I promise, no one wants to exclude you." I couldn't help but suspect her fingers were crossed behind her back even though we were on the phone. "Mike's cousin and wife are taking our room, I'm taking the couch. I thought you'd prefer the privacy of a hotel room! Would you rather sleep on the couch?"

"What did you say to Sheila?"

"Nothing. Not one thing. You're paranoid, Ian. I begged you to stay on the Zoloft." I could visualize Gillian talking into the receiver, sighing in frustration, but also satisfied that I was reacting in exactly the way she must have predicted.

"My dick won't work on that stuff. Not that I've had a chance to use it anytime in the last three years."

"I still have to come down to Arkansas for you to sign the paperwork. We can talk about everything then."

"Absolutely," I said. "Come on down. I can't fucking wait."

Later, after I had calmed down, I called Mike and told him I needed to stay home and write this year. I lied and told him I'd been banging away on a novel since I'd moved to Russellville and I couldn't afford to take a break. Truth was I hadn't written a word in months.

"It won't be the same without you to make the martinis, man," Mike had said, his voice a strange mix of relief and regret. "You're hell on that shaker." My secret wasn't the shaker. My secret was that I "washed" the brine off the olives by sucking on them.

"I taught Gillian everything I know," I said, but I knew she wouldn't put the olives in her mouth and lovingly clean them with her tongue. She found this practice, and the rest of my habits, undignified.

"No hard feelings?"

"Don't be silly," I said. "I've got work to do. It's just one of those things nobody can help." I secretly wished a nor'easter would roll in and drown the lot of them. Eventually I became so sick with resentment, I bought a propane fish fryer and a croquet set and decided to throw a party of my own.

I'd erected the croquet set with perfect symmetry, measuring the distance between wickets with my Stanley Lock tape measure. But in the hard light of the morning, when I walked out onto the front porch, it looked like a crew of gremlins had wreaked havoc on the lawn. There were huge divots eaten into the freshly mowed zoysia and tire tracks at the edge of the yard; some of the wickets were bent and others were missing. Mallets and balls were scattered across the lawn in cryptic disarray, as if the pattern of their arrangement might make a picture or spell out a word, if I only had the strength to climb onto the roof or scale a tall pine. But from the porch, the code of remaining stakes, wickets, colored balls, and mallets was an indecipherable mystery.

I sat down in one of the folding chairs and breathed deeply from my diaphragm, the way the counselor at school had taught me. I closed my eyes and placed the tip of my tongue on the back of my teeth. I took a deep breath and held it for a seven count. The panic wasn't new. In fact, the panic was the one constant left in my life that I could rely on. The first attack had come barreling down on me like a bear out of the woods. I'd thought I was having a heart attack and made Gillian drive me four blocks to the Good Samaritan emergency room, the whole time shaking her head behind the wheel in silence.

The triage nurse at Good Sam took my blood pressure and blinked. "Have you been taking cocaine?"

"No."

"Your blood pressure is 180 over 110. You're only twenty-seven years old."

"I'm terrified," I said, clutching my chest.

"Of what, honey?" She gave me a sympathetic wince and patted my arm.

At the touch of her warm hand on my skin, tears welled up in my eyes. "I honestly don't know."

But I guess that wasn't really the truth. My dissertation was due at the end of the year, my funding was running out, I still had yet to pass my foreign-language exam, the job market for new professors in English had taken another sharp downturn, my father was dying of CLL leukemia far away in another state, and I knew deep in my heart that sometime within the last two years my wife had stopped loving me, but for the life of me I couldn't pinpoint just when. The fluctuating stock market of my courage had just crashed and I felt like jumping out a window.

I cursed Dawson, Surge, and Finney for raiding my tranquilizers. My grad students were self-indulgent, cavalier little prepschoolers from the Mississippi Delta, too smart and lazy for the farm. They got hopped up on ADD medication to speed through their morning classes and smoked pot openly on their porches in the afternoons to come down. In the Delta, it was a simple fact that white people didn't go to jail. So they lived as if an ambient halo of invulnerability surrounded them, even though Dawson already had one DUI from the western part of the state and Finney had been arrested for putting a skinny biker in the hospital, the result of a petty squabble over Bruce Springsteen.

Their daddies were all rich. They had either inherited acre upon acre of fertile, black topsoil, or they worked as modern-day corporate overseers, racists with cell phones ordering the "niggers" to and fro on a speedy fleet of John Deeres. In truth, though, I found the whole spoiled lot of my rotten students charming. Had I been any different a few short years ago, before the old man took sick and my beautiful wife, with her swanlike grace, turned as cold as an ice sculpture? Still, I knew there was a day of reckoning coming for the kids, when a black cloud of sorrow would inevitably storm up over their heads and they would no longer be able to run between the rain drops. If it didn't happen sooner rather than later, they would either get themselves killed or wind up in rehab.

That's when it occurred to me—perhaps their reckoning had already come, in the wee hours of the morning. A fresh wave of panic washed over me. Maybe one of them had crashed going home from my party. An ugly image shattered my front-porch meditation. I could see it all before me, the state trooper's blue lights illuminating the twisted wreckage of an SUV. The police would probably think I had given them the painkillers willingly. It would all end five years from now with me being shot down for tenure. Maybe the head wouldn't even wait for tenure. Perhaps he would simply dismiss me out of hand, invoke the "moral turpitude" clause in my contract and then bam—terminated. Perhaps even a rich Delta daddy would turn one of his high-powered lawyers on me. Was prison out of the question? I ran into the house and started making calls.

After trying everyone's number twice, I finally roused Dawson. "I was just checking to see if y'all had made it home all right."

"Sho' nuff, G." He giggled, mock gangster. I was grateful to hear his smart-assery again.

"You doing all right?"

"Yeah. I got a big mess to clean, and I'm hungover. I think a cat took a shit in my mouth while I was asleep. Hey, did you take any pills out of my medicine cabinet?"

"Uh, I think Surge did. He's been speeding all week."

"Do you know if he made it home? You're the only one I can get on the phone."

"He slept on my couch."

"He can't take my pills like that," I said. "I need those. The doctor gave me those for a reason."

"You're nervous, right?"

"I prefer to think of myself as high-strung."

"I thought after last night you'd be hiding in your closet with a flashlight."

I stopped, took a deep breath, and tried to slow my brain down enough to sift through the events of the past evening. I had started prepping for the party at midafternoon. Surge had brought twenty pounds of frozen whole catfish, and I watched with admiration as he defrosted them in the cooler with a garden hose and expertly filleted the goggle-eyed creatures in the back yard. Then Surge hooked up the fish fryer to the propane tank with a crescent wrench. I had worried at first about putting a speed freak in charge of something as volatile as pressurized pro-pane, but he operated the fryer with all the expert skill he'd used to fillet the fish. I'd never met someone who stayed up for days on end who had such a steady hand. By then the other guests had started to arrive, many bringing dishes of homemade potato salad, coleslaw, fresh blueberries, and lemon icebox pie. We set up a serving line off the tailgate of my truck under the canopy of the carport.

Most of the guests were grad students and professors from the English, history, and foreign-language departments, but a few of the waitresses I chatted with at the Holiday Inn Lounge, the only private club in this dry county, came too. As the attendance swelled, we ate slowly and with relish, occasionally stopping by the inflatable swimming pool I had filled with ice and beer. I re-membered that in the early hours of the party, despite all the good cheer around me, I couldn't keep my mind off the cabin in Rodanthe. This fish fry was just a cheap imitation of the grilled steaks and chilled martinis that Gillian, Mike, and the rest were enjoying on the cool, windswept beach. My natural tendency toward melancholy and resentment refused to evaporate in the bright afternoon sunshine. But as dusk settled, my mood became more carefree. I lit the tiki torches and we began a round of croquet in the glow of tribal flames.

I had to explain the game to many of the guests. There was a zaftig blonde undergrad named Lizzy Crumb, a former student from my very first creative-writing class, who had hitched a ride with some of the waitresses from the lounge. I wasn't really comfortable with her being there at first, but she was maybe twenty-two or twenty-three and wasn't drinking, so I didn't have the heart to ask her to leave. After I got used to the idea of having her there, I took special pleasure in coaching her around the wickets, showing her how to line up shots and collect extra strokes. She almost won, too, but one of the full professors outfoxed us in the end.

From her poems I knew she was from Vicksburg, Mississippi, a city on the lip of the Delta, and I thought maybe she had taken time out of school to go to work or perhaps even rehab. At the end of the semester, she had turned in a short story called "The Summer It Snowed" about two lovers from Vicksburg who had spent a whole summer living in the home of a young widow. The widow had just collected on a massive life-insurance policy, and the flood of new money turned her into a cocaine shut-in who rarely left the warm waters of her kidney-shaped swimming pool. She used the lovers as couriers; every night she gave them enough cash for a couple of eight balls, and they stayed up until dawn, snorting in their bathing suits—wet, chatty, and high.

Around ten o'clock most of the professors headed for home, all of them except the one who'd won the first round of croquet. He was a gray-bearded bachelor, an ex-hippy, a civil-rights protester from back in the day.

"This is the first party we've had that's been worth a damn

here for ten years," he said, swirling his scotch around in his high-ball glass.

"Glad you're having a good time. More ice?"

He shook his head. "What's wrong with the other people your age? All they want to do is play with their kids."

"I don't know," I said. "When I was a student, we hung out with professors all the time. We went to bars together. Their wives invited us to their homes for dinner." I shrugged and topped off his glass. "Everybody's so litigious these days; I guess nobody thinks a party is worth it."

"A good party is what separates us from the animals."

Just short of midnight, I spied the full prof and Dawson sequestered away in my laundry room eating mushrooms out of a Ziploc bag. The drunken waitresses had cleared space in the living room. One of them had brought over a CD of early-sixties' beach music, and she was showing the others how to shag. Over the music I could hear Surge and Finney arguing seriously about what possums eat. I had long forgotten Lizzy Crumb when I discovered her kneeling on the floor of my bedroom, looking at the books on the shelves.

"Hey," I said. "What are you up to in here all alone? Aren't you having fun?" I walked into the room and sat down on the bed, but left the door wide open.

She gave me a long hard look like she was trying to make her mind up about something. "I was supposed to be at home with my boyfriend tonight. It's our two-year anniversary." She looked up and gave me a disappointed smile.

"What's the matter?"

She shrugged. "Hey, you have a first edition of Denis Johnson's *Jesus' Son.*"

"Yep," I stood up and plucked the book off the shelf. "Signed, too. My friend Vivé studied with him in Austin. She sent it to me." I handed the book to her so she could read the inscription: "To Ian—Looking forward to reading your work." For the first time in hours my thoughts turned to the cabin in Rodanthe. I wondered if Vivé had made the pilgrimage all the way from Texas. I wondered if she missed me, or if she was glad I wasn't there.

"How neat. That's my favorite book."

"Didn't we read one of his stories in our class?"

Lizzy nodded. "'Emergency.' I'd never heard of him before then."

"It's a pretty great book. Why don't we go back and join the rest of the party?" I held my hand out to help her up off the floor. I could see her delicate bare feet sticking out of the folds of her skirt and I wondered where her shoes were. "Here," I said. "I'll show you how to make a martini."

"Okay," she said sliding up to me. Her cloudy blue eyes rose up to meet mine, and I was pleasantly surprised to discover that we were exactly the same height. Gillian had been a full three inches taller than me, and I had always wondered if this increased her ability to intimidate me. "But just one drink," said Lizzy. "I have to drive all of those beachcombers home."

Back in the kitchen, I showed her how I coated the martini glass with vermouth and poured the excess out, since most people preferred their martinis dry. "King Eider vermouth is best," I said. "But it's hard to come by here in a dry county in Arkansas." She lifted up a martini glass of her own and imitated the ritual, swishing a capful of the amber liquid around the bowl of the crystal. Then I poured a generous helping of gin in the shaker. "Here, you shake," I said.

"How long?"

"'Til your hands are so cold you can't take it anymore."

Lizzy held the shaker over her head and began to sing "La Cucaracha," using the shaker for a marimba. Her ample body jiggled pleasantly.

"The secret," I said, "is cleaning the brine off the olives with your mouth." I opened a jar of Krinos Green Cracked Olives from the fridge and placed one on my tongue. She stopped shaking for a moment and opened her mouth. I placed an olive on her tongue.

"Don't worry," I mumbled, working my tongue around the green flesh. "The alcohol kills any germs."

She stepped closer to me, sucking sweetly, her mouth sewn up in a tart pucker. "I'm not worried."

I chastely pressed my lips to hers, our tongues both still rolling around the olives. Her lips tasted sweetly of mentholated cigarettes and sugar-fried hush puppies.

Beyond that first martini, my memories slurred into a jumbled mess. Was it just the one kiss or had I made out with her in front of my colleague, the grad students, the waitresses? Had I attempted to take her to bed? If I had, rumors would already be spreading through our tiny town like a virus.

"Yo G, you still there?"

"Yeah," I said, my limbic system radiating waves of fear. "Just barely."

According to Dawson, he was the only one who saw me kiss Lizzy in the kitchen. But somehow I couldn't bring myself to be relieved. I spent the better part of the morning collecting garbage and washing dishes, taking intermittent breaks to reproach myself. I had to be more careful. I was desperately lonely, yes, but there was no loophole for the brokenhearted in my employment contract. What if I lost my job? Who would take care of my mother? My dad had left me in charge of that on his deathbed— "Son, take care of your mother," he'd said in his kind, paternal way. "I'm not going to be here, but I know I can count on you. You've never let me down." I had let him down plenty of times, but his willingness to forget about the ignominies of my childhood had made me want to embrace him, or at least hold his hand. My God, why hadn't I?

When all the surfaces were cleared away, I took another look at the yard. A bright dew of uneasiness glistened on the grass. Again it seemed as if some message concerning my fate was spelled out on the green postcard of my lawn, only it was written in an occult alphabet. Instead of ripping up the stakes and wickets, I decided to put a load of clothes in the wash and go back to bed. Sometime around noon, there was a knock on my door. I opened it to find Lizzy's freckled smile lighting up my doorstep. She was wearing a summery white spaghetti-strap blouse that exposed her milky shoulders.

"I'm going to see my parents in the 'Burg today. Want to come?"

"Hey, I don't know if I did or said anything last night—"

Lizzy held up her hand and smirked. "You were a blast. A total blast. But from what you told me, you could use a vacation."

"What did I tell you?"

"You told me I was the first woman to make you happy in three years," she blinked flirtatiously. "You asked me to marry you in Vegas—you know, when your divorce comes through. Don't you remember?"

"Vegas?" I blushed. Despite the ache in my muscles, I couldn't help but feel exhilarated by her presence. "Did I really say that?"

"I'm a counselor at the Salvation Army Summer Camp and I have to be back there by this time tomorrow, so I have to come back and spend the night here. I just thought you could use a day trip. What's the worst that could happen?"

Another car-wreck movie played in my mind, questions arising as to why I was in a car with a student, irate parents, irate administrators. I thought of my widowed mother, shaking her head in disgrace. My father looking down from heaven, saintly tears of blood dripping onto his celestial white robe.

"What about your boyfriend?" I asked.

"We broke up after I got home last night. This time for good. He only wants me around when it's convenient for him. I'm moving my stuff out when the lease is up."

"Don't you think your parents will find meeting me a little weird?"

"You don't know my parents," she said giggling, twisting her patchwork skirt with her fingers. "They'll love you." I looked down at her feet to see her pink toes.

"Do you ever wear shoes?"

She scrunched up her face. "I have flip-flops in the car if my feet bother you."

"No. They don't bother me." It amused me to think of prim Gillian. Oh, the face she would make at the folks who perambulated barefoot in Wal-Mart.

"Let me put my clothes in the dryer," I said. "Then we'll go."

Twenty minutes later we were hurtling eastward toward Little Rock, the landscape flush with kudzu and loblolly pines. Lizzy kept one of her bare feet on the accelerator, pressed dangerously close to the floorboard; the other was propped out the window. I tried my best not to stare at the porcelain curvature of her thigh.

Occasionally Lizzy would smile at me, let go of the wheel completely, and use both hands to light a Salem. When she did this, my heart would flutter up in my throat like a terrified dove. I could see it pleased her to shake me up.

"What do your parents do?" I asked.

"My dad's a gunsmith." She said.

"Great. He's probably going to take one look at me and shoot me right in the head."

Lizzy giggled. "No. He's not like that. He doesn't even like to hunt. He just likes the precision of it. It's all a puzzle to him. He plays golf in his spare time. The hunters love him, though. Come winter the fridge is full of venison steaks. The cops love him, too. He's got some sort of contract with the both the PD and the sheriff's department."

"Did he go to school to learn to do that?"

"No. He's the smartest man I know, but he didn't go to school. He worked on planes in the Air Force and when he came home, he pretty much taught himself. He can fix antique clocks, too, but there's not as much call for that in the 'Burg."

"What's your mom like?"

Lizzy shook her head. "She's not from Mississippi. She's from Dayton. They eloped when he was in the military." She paused. "Hey—can I ask you something? What happened with you and your wife?"

I was surprised by how much the question hurt. I looked out the window and took the time to count five snowy egrets standing on the back of a Holstein heifer as we passed by her pasture.

"We lost our balance. My dad was sick for a long time, and I turned into a hypochondriac. I just couldn't believe I wasn't dying, too. I saw the doctor two or three times a month just to hear

134

him tell me I was okay. I turned into the kind of person that flinches at unexpected noises. The coffeepot was always on. Every time I left my apartment, I had these weird fantasies that the building was burning down in my absence. I guess my nerves got on her nerves. She came down here last week and we signed the papers. Now all we have left is to see the judge." I twisted my wedding ring round and round with my thumb. "Uh, what about you? Why the breakup?"

"Jack's a mechanical kind of guy like my dad, but not as laid-back. Jack thinks he's got all the angles figured, including me. He doesn't respect me either. In fact, one time I came home and found an equation at the bottom of one of my stories. Under it he'd typed, 'If you can solve this you will have my respect.' I printed out the equation, wrote '= Fuck You' and slipped it into one of his engineering textbooks. What a prick!" Lizzy lit up another cigarette and puffed, agitated.

"Did y'all really live with a coke addict for a whole summer?"

Now it was Lizzy's turn to look pained, to take a moment and brace for whatever confession would come next. "Yeah. That's another reason I broke up with him. He got me into all of that shit. It was his friend's mom, and we lived at her house with our noses in a sugar bowl for two months. My head's still fucked up from that. I don't sleep right anymore. You know they cut coke with ethyl. Every time I fill up the car now, the smell of gasoline makes me gag. I can feel gas dripping in the back of my throat. Every time I look at Jack—" She shook her head and shuddered. "I've just got to get away from him."

"So you want to be a writer?"

"Kind of. I want to be a photojournalist. But they don't have a class for that at Tech." Lizzy hiked her thumb toward the back seat. An expensive looking Nikon with a long, snouty lens rested in the back. "Some of my photos of Vicksburg are up in the Corps of Engineering offices."

"Impressive."

"Well, I'm sure my mother had something to do with it. She's been working there as a secretary for years."

We exited off the interstate and onto the highway that runs through the small towns of Marvel and Brinkley; sometime before we crossed the bridge over the Mississippi in West Helena, we stopped to gas up the car. Lizzy bought a pack of Salems and a Monterey cigar.

"What's with the stogie? A gift for your dad?"

"Not my dad. My friend Heather's dad. I promised we'd drop by her house."

I offered to pay for her gas, but she wouldn't let me.

"I'll put it on the Shell card. My folks pick up the bill."

I shrugged and toddled off to the men's room. On the way back, I realized that I had forgotten to brush my teeth that morning and my mouth was still cottony. I could taste the tartar on the backs of my teeth. I went to the aisle behind the candy and bought a toothbrush, paste, and a small bottle of off-brand mouthwash called Dr. Tichenor's. The slogan on the bottle read, "It Not Only Kills Germs, It Goes After Their Families."

As we moved past the river and took Highway 61 south, the kudzu took on a lusher hue of green; its poisonous-looking vines now drowned a few abandoned houses as well as the pines. In the air was the semimetallic smell of cotton poison and defoliant. When we arrived at the edge of Vicksburg, it was hard to distinguish it from most other American towns, with its McDonald's and Kentucky Fried Chicken, but the city had made something of an industry of its Civil War past. Billboards directed tourists to monuments and historic cemeteries. The other major industry was gambling.

"I worked there in high school." Lizzy pointed at a billboard for the Battlefield Inn. "I wore a hoop skirt behind the counter. Can you believe that?"

"I bet you looked like a real southern belle. Do you like to go out to the casino and play the slots?"

"No, I never win anything. I don't have that kind of luck."

"What are you going to do for fun when we elope to Vegas? Maybe you'll wear the hoop skirt as a wedding gown."

"Aw, Ian," Lizzy looked over her shoulder, and then shifted into the left lane to pass a rickety Buick. "I outgrew that thing years ago." As if to brace herself for the acceleration, she clamped her hand down on my knee and floored it.

Evidently a good gunsmith can make a make quite a living in Mississippi. Lizzy's house stood just off Highway 80. It was a spacious Tudor with a huge pool and a guest house. We spent an hour or so talking with her mother. Her living room was filled with all manner of antique clocks, whirling and spinning around our heads. There was also a miniature village in the foyer that looked like something displayed in the window of a toy store in an old movie: there was a post office, a train station, a lighthouse. The detail was amazing. "Lizzy's dad made that for her when she was a little girl," her mother told me shortly after our introduction. Through the window of one of the miniature homes I spied a tiny *Life* magazine about the size of a postage stamp on the tiny coffee table. Mrs. Crumb ("call me Linda") was a young-looking woman with an Oil of Olay complexion. When she extended her hand to mine, it felt cool and smooth as lotion. She had not lost her neutral midwestern accent, which was so soft and plain, it almost made her seem exotic.

"It's so nice to meet one of Lizzy's friends from school. She enjoyed your class so much. She used to call and tell me about it in the afternoons."

Blood rushed to my face. I felt naked. If she could only read my thoughts, she'd never stop slapping me. "Liz is very bright," I said. "I was lucky to have her."

"Lizzy told me you were recently divorced?"

I was taken aback. Lizzy had called and told her mother this? When? Last night? This morning? "Yes," I admitted. "We filed the paperwork a few days ago."

"I'm sorry to hear that. Life doesn't always work out the way we plan."

You said it, sister, I thought. This trip was proof of that.

"Where's Daddy?" asked Lizzy.

"Where he always is. At work."

"Well, I want to take Ian to meet Heather."

"Be home for dinner by seven. Your father wants to meet the young professor here."

"Okay, okay," she said. We'd no sooner closed the door than she gave a sigh of exasperation.

"What?" I said. "She's sweet. Still, don't you think she thinks it's weird that we're here together? I can't believe you told her I was getting divorced."

Lizzy waved her hand dismissively. "She thinks you're a catch."

We got back in the car. As she closed the door, Lizzy's face took on a bold but wicked determination, as if she were about to challenge me to a duel or a game of chicken. "Look," she said.

"I've been at Christian camp all month. I haven't been laid or high in three weeks. Something's got to give."

"Meaning what, exactly?"

"Either we go to the Battlefield Inn and fuck our brains out, or we go to Heather's and we get stoned."

I had no interest in getting stoned. Pot made me more paranoid than usual. But at least if we were caught, it probably wouldn't make the papers in Arkansas. The crime might stay hidden in Mississippi. If I had sex with her, that would follow me to school; it would follow me for the rest of my life. I would officially be in league with the fraternity of lecherous old men who slept with their students, an organization I had always despised. If I smoked marijuana with Lizzy Crumb, that would be a crime, yes. But if I had sex with Lizzy Crumb, that would be a sin. Only I longed desperately to be a sinner.

"Lizzy, this field trip is bad enough. If I got caught having an affair with a student—"

"I haven't been in one of your classes for eight months. What are you worried about? It's not even against the rules."

"It's kind of frowned upon."

Lizzy gave a derisive snort, already punching numbers on her cell phone. "Heather," she said, "I'm in town, and I'm bringing a friend."

When we drove up to the house, we found Heather in the backyard hanging laundry out to dry. A beautiful slip of a girl, Heather was blond and freckled like Lizzy, but more tan, a bit slimmer in the hips and bosom. I watched as she stood on her tiptoes to pin a white bedsheet to the wire, her slick calf muscle flexing up to the back of her knee.

"Hey," Lizzy called.

Heather careened her head, finished pinning the sheet, and then ran toward her friend, tackling her with a warm hug. When she arose from Lizzy's neck she turned to face me.

"He's cute. Is he really your professor?"

Lizzy giggled. She must have phoned her friend and told her about me right after she called her mom. I could see now that this must have been part of Lizzy's attraction to me, showing me off. It made me feel like an exotic pet on a leash.

"We just had one class together. It's summer," she said sarcastically. "He's not *my* anything."

"Don't you have a dryer?" I asked Heather.

"Sure. But the clothes smell better sun-dried."

"Where's your dad?" asked Lizzy. "I was hoping he could roll us up a blunt." Lizzy produced a gray-and-black 35-millimeter-film canister. She opened the top. It was full of marijuana.

"You had that in the car with us the whole time?"

Lizzy grinned.

"Let's go inside," said Heather. "I have to put in another load of clothes."

"Your dad smokes with you?" I asked in utter disbelief.

"No, he says it doesn't do much for him anymore. But he's a head from way back. In high school, he'd always roll up our joints for us. I do a sloppy job. But he got called into work, so I'll see what I can do."

We walked inside. Strangely, the interior of the house seemed bigger than the outside. Heather's dad was obviously a pack rat. His living room looked like a flea market, every nook and cranny filled with collectable junk: Civil War figurines, funeral-home fans, antique lamps, lunch boxes, yardsticks, Depression glass, green bank ledgers, even a taxidermied beaver sitting atop a huge black gun safe. In the center of it all was a wide-screen TV that cast a menacingly modern light on the dusty armoire and the duct-taped La-Z-Boy recliner.

I watched with rapt fascination as the two young women set to work. Lizzy industriously separated the stems and seeds from the leaves of the marijuana, and Heather removed the tobacco from the cigar. Heather got up to put more clothes in the washer, and when she returned we went outside to the back of the house to smoke. The two girls sat on deck chairs while I perched on a riding lawnmower parked under the second-story deck. I watched them pass the blunt back and forth as I gathered up the courage to take a hit myself. I'd never smoked a blunt before, only a few hits of a joint or two at the end of some college party, always resulting in an ugly case of the bed spins. I thought it might be different this time. Mainly I just didn't want to look square. I took the smoke deep into my lungs and held it, and then exhaled, fighting the urge to cough.

The girls chattered away about Vicksburg gossip. They uttered the names of a whole society of strangers, their fights and falling-outs, their secrets, their love affairs. It was like watching a soap opera for the first time. Eventually Lizzy and Heather became hard to understand, their dialogue jumbled and difficult to process, as if they were on the front seat of a jerky roller coaster and I was in back trying to eavesdrop on their conversation as the ride veered up and down, side to side. When the blunt was half dead, Lizzy asked for a shotgun.

Heather clapped her hands. "Oh, we haven't done that for such a long time."

They stood face to face, each girl putting one end of the blunt between her lips. Heather blew through the cigar tubing, piping

141

a huge plume of smoke down Lizzy's throat. Lizzy returned the favor. For a heart-stopping moment their mouths were so close I thought they might push their lips together in a fiery kiss.

"Okay," said Heather, pinching the nub of the blunt between her thumb and forefinger. "I need to take my clothes off now."

What? I thought. Only I must have said it out loud. The girls began to shiver with peals of hysterical laughter, tears rolling down their cheeks. Blood rushed to my face as they pointed their fingers at me, stumbled, staggered, hugged, and laughed some more.

"No, silly," said Heather, gasping for air. "I mean take the wash off the line."

"I think I'm going to pee myself." Lizzy crossed her legs.

That's when I started to giggle and couldn't stop. That's when I started to have a good time.

My good time was short lived. Half an hour later, I urged Lizzy to get me the hell out of there as a dark cloud of paranoia settled over me and I realized I was about to freak out. Trussed up snuggly in the seat belt of Lizzy's car, I suddenly lost the ability to complete my thoughts. I mumbled and stuttered incoherently. Half-formed ideas evaporated like soap bubbles before they reached my tongue. I had a headache. My hands trembled. My eyes felt too big for my skull. From my heart to my testicles, my internal organs were filled with quick-drying cement. Cockroaches ran through the wet cardboard of my brain.

"Oh my God, Oh my God, Oh my God."

"Are you okay?" Lizzy looked at me, genuine concern on her face.

"Liz," I said. "I can't meet your father like this."

"Honey, you're just really stoned. It's only five o'clock. We'll drive around until you feel better."

I couldn't imagine ever being straight again, much less being straight enough to eat dinner with Lizzy's parents in two hours.

"How?"

"How what?"

"How can you drive like this?"

"Practice makes perfect. I drive better stoned than sober. I don't speed."

We drove all over Vicksburg, from the suburbs to the old downtown. Most of the trip was a blur. I do remember the places Lizzy said were her favorites to photograph, the grand Vicksburg Hotel and a bar called the Biscuit Company. We drove through National Monument Park, where the ghosts of the war dead seemed to linger around battlefield markers. We drove through a long, winding cemetery full of gothic headstones and family plots where several generations were entombed. Lizzy pointed out her grandfather's grave. I laughed and wept intermittently. When I laughed she laughed with me and when I cried she held my hand. Occasionally she apologized, "Ian, I'm so, so sorry. I didn't know the weed would do this to you." I realized when she said it that never once during the entire course of our marriage had Gillian ever apologized for anything.

My mouth was filmy with cannabis resin. I had yet to brush my teeth. It suddenly became imperative that I get the taste of marijuana out of my mouth. I ordered Lizzy to stop the car on the edge of the cemetery drive and park under a tall, tortured oak.

"Where, where did she put my mouthwash," I mumbled.

"You want me to do what to your mouth?"

"My mouthwash," I said. "I want to use my mouthwash." Lizzy informed me the paper bag I had brought out of the gas station with me was in the back seat. I took off my seat belt, grabbed the bag, fished out the tiny bottle of Dr. Tichenor's and upended it, expecting the cool, refreshing bite of something like Listerine. But Dr. Tichenor's was more like mineral spirits. I opened the car door and spewed the chemical mix onto the grass. "Liz," I whimpered, "I don't think that was mouthwash. I think I put shoe polish or something in my mouth." The interior of my palate was stripped bare. My lungs burned as if I'd inhaled an accelerant. If someone had lit a match, I would have spit fire all over the dashboard.

Lizzy went epileptic with laughter. When she finally managed to breathe, she snatched the bottle of Dr. Tichenor's from my hand and said, "I don't think you're supposed to drink this straight. See?" She pointed to the back label: "Dilute with water."

That's when the blue lights flickered behind us.

"Oh Jesus," I said. Only it was an actual appeal to heaven rather than a curse.

"Just be cool," Lizzy said, still unable to keep a straight face.

A black-and-white patrol car eased up behind us.

We sat in purgatory for what seemed like millennia before a mustached officer of about twenty-five finally got out of his car and leisurely made his way to the driver's window. Lizzy rolled down the window. "Hi."

The officer stuck his head in the door and immediately crinkled his nose. "Good God a'mighty, what have y'all been drinking? It smells like Pine Sol in here."

I started to mumble something about Dr. Tichenor.

"Who?"

"This asshole is drunk." Lizzy pointed an accusatory finger at me. "I found him at the Casino bar ready to pass out. We have to have dinner with my parents at seven o'clock and he's so drunk he can't hardly talk. He lost a whole week's pay, too." Lizzy pummeled me in the upper body with all the fury of a welterweight.

"Hey, hey." The cop grabbed her arm, wrinkling his nose in disgust, disappointed to be involved in yet another domestic dispute. He sighed. "Let me see your license."

Lizzy grabbed her purse and plucked out her wallet. I wondered if there were any more film canisters of cannabis inside Lizzy's handbag. The officer inspected the license carefully and then Lizzy's face.

"Do you have any drugs in the car? Y'all wouldn't have come out to the graveyard to get high, would you?"

There was a tense moment of silence when all I could hear was the irregular beats of my defibrillating heart.

"Officer, to tell you the truth," Lizzy opened up her purse, "I have this." She showed him the film canister; there couldn't have been more than a pinch of weed left. "I was so mad at him." She hiked her thumb at me for emphasis. "I was gonna smoke it to calm down, but there's not enough." Lizzy handed the officer the canister and he peered inside. "Please don't bust us. This was the first time he was going to meet my parents and now everything is ruined, just ruined." Lizzy began to sob. "My daddy's going to kill me."

Lizzy wept openly. Were these real? If not, she was a hell of an actor. Finally, the cop glared back down at the license. Then his face softened, "Hey, your daddy isn't Danny Crumb, the gunsmith, is he?"

Lizzy looked up innocently and sniffed, "Why, yes, sir, he is."

The cop simply confiscated Lizzy's film canister and wrote her a warning ticket for loitering. I suspected that this wasn't the first time Lizzy had dodged trouble because of who her father was. We were late for dinner, but only by half an hour. The adrenaline released during our encounter with Vicksburg's finest somewhat cleared the fog from my brain, but reentering the Crumb home with its whirling clocks and its miniature village made me feel like an anachronistic Gulliver among the Lilliputians.

That was until I met the Brobdingnagian Danny Crumb, who towered over me. Contrary to my expectations, his handshake was firm and reassuring, a lever that seemed to pry open his smiling face. "Nice to meet you," he said, peering down at me through coke-bottle bifocals.

"You too," I said looking up to him, somewhat unwilling to release his hand.

"There's pizza and paper plates on the counter," Lizzy's mother informed us. "Are you hungry?"

Lizzy rubbed her stomach. "Starved."

There was a portable TV on the counter, and we gathered round to watch a sci-fi show. I suddenly felt ravenous, and I ate slice after slice, enjoying the way my numb stomach expanded to make room for my gluttony. Halfway through the meal, a commercial came on the television encouraging vacationers to visit Las Vegas, with the promising slogan, "What Happens in Vegas, Stays in Vegas." Lizzy and I exchanged glances. Linda fluttered about the kitchen, freshening drinks and eventually clearing the counter.

Though Danny Crumb said little, there was something about him that seemed to loan me part of his quiet confidence. Like many men of a mechanical bent, he saw no reason to fill up the room with empty chatter. He asked me no questions about my work or about how I knew Lizzy. I'm sure he had been well informed by Lizzy's mother by now. The world ticked along without the grease of conversation. I suspected he knew we were high, but if he did he kept this fact to himself; not so much as a wrinkle of disappointment or judgment creased his face. Though I myself was used to talking through an awkward situation, I was scared to say much, afraid I might blurt out something that would be both eggheaded and stupid, something like, *You know, possums are the only North American marsupials,* or *It's ironic that the Holy Roman Empire was neither Holy nor Roman,* or *It's a little known fact, I'm totally head-over-heels in love with your daughter.*

After a couple of beers, Danny Crumb began to tell his family about his day during the commercials. He recollected the customers that came in and out, the sale of an expensive rifle, the minute calibrations needed to repair a damaged pistol, a knock-knock joke told by a Vicksburg deputy. That's when it came to me. This man is happy. And why not? He has weight and importance in the world. He is a man who can fix things. Even time bends to his fingers. He has gone about the business of marrying a beautiful wife and raising an equally beautiful daughter. The daughter has brought home a suitor, a professor at the university not far from home. All is right with the world. What could be simpler?

"Do you own a gun, Ian?"

His face was so serene, it was a wonder he had any reason to even speak to me at all.

"My father left me his pistol when he passed away, a .22 magnum, Sentinel Mark IV. It probably hasn't been fired since he got sick."

Danny nodded in sympathy. "Has he been gone long?"

"A little more than a year."

"It's hard losing your dad. I still miss mine."

I was sorry to bring the pall of death to the dinner table. But before I knew it, the lugubrious moment had passed. Lizzy and her mom made plans for another wave of renovations for the house: saloon doors for the kitchen, old bricks and a sugar kettle for the backyard. Danny sat back and listened to the way they would spend his money, smiling. I sat back and watched him smile. When we readied ourselves to leave, Lizzy hugged her parents. Linda hugged me. Danny shook my hand. Before letting me go, he moved toward me one inch closer. "Come see us again, fella." There was a squint of sincerity. Then a final shake from side to side, like a tiller.

"I will." I realized then that I wasn't only smitten with Lizzy, I was in love with her whole family.

For a while we drove in satisfied silence. Groggy with bread and cheese, I settled into what turned out to be an uneasy slumber. All the way from Little Rock to Russellville, I dreamed that my house had burned to the ground in my absence. The lint filter in my dryer had caught fire and the flames had licked their way up the walls and to the roof. I woke to a flash of red lights and sirens, but it was only a passing ambulance. My heart thudded against my chest. Then Lizzy's hand was shaking my shoulder. "Get up, sweetie," she said. "You're home."

I rubbed my eyes for a long time and stared at the cool, dark windows of my house. I unbuckled my seat belt and turned to face Lizzy to say goodnight. Before I knew what had happened, she was kissing me, and to my dread pleasure I found that I was kissing her back. Angry with her for arousing me, I squeezed her waist, clawed her back, pinched her breasts and thighs. Three years of unrequited lust overpowered me. I kissed her with all the self-destructive rage of a burning building. At that moment I loved her, loved her so much I wanted to put my hands on her throat and strangle her. Good God. I pulled myself away and lurched for the door handle.

Lizzy grabbed my shoulder. "A goodnight kiss? That's all I get?" She looked hurt and puzzled. "But it will be another three weeks before Salvation Army camp is over."

"I wish I could invite you in. Forgive me, but the sad fact is— I'm still technically married." I held up my wedding band. "Besides," I placed her hand on my chest so she could feel my palpitating heart. "You scare me to death." I got out of the car and stumbled across the obstacle course of my lawn, dodging wickets and colored balls, feeling every bit as beat-up as the wrecked turf.

That will have been a year ago tomorrow. I did eventually make love to Lizzy. When my divorce came through and my courage returned, we had a sweet and tender affair that lasted until the start of the spring semester. I spent Christmas Eve at Danny and Linda's house, exchanging gifts in front of the miniature village, which Lizzy's father had equipped with artificial snow and electric lights. A few weeks later, Lizzy dropped out of school and eloped with her ex-boyfriend, not to Vegas but to Charleston, though I have heard through Heather that she has already filed papers and will soon join the ranks of the divorced.

For the first week after she married, I fantasized about suicide like a sullen teenager and dreamed about the people who would line up to weep at my funeral. Mostly I just liked having an excuse to hold my father's pistol; no doubt it will remain unloaded. I am better now, though I have resorted to occasionally snorting my Lorazepam in the dark hours of morning when the questions descend on me like bats. What was I to her? Why did she marry someone else? Did she ever love me? I wonder. I wonder.

Tonight I am throwing a party to take my mind off her. I have erected a new croquet set with my trusty Stanley Lock tape measure, and soon Dawson, Surge, and Finney will be here with catfish and drugs.

Still, I wish she'd read this and give me a call.

The Bear Bryant Funeral Train

Today one of the secretaries brought out a little white cake with candles and my name written on it. Then she got on the intercom and led the whole Vance Mercedes factory in a rendition of "For He's a Jolly Good Fellow." The song, like my retirement, was a bit forced. But some of my engineering friends brought gifts.

"How about this!" cried Doogie Sims, brandishing a stainless-steel Sabatier meat cleaver high in the air. I pretended to cringe in fear, and then we laughed. Cleve Weathers brought me a bottle of Laugavulin Scotch with a red bow tied to the cork. "I thought they'd have to drag you out of the labs in a body bag," he said. Everyone laughed.

The guys on the assembly line got together and framed a poster of the 1934 Crimson Tide team at the Rose Bowl, the one with the dapper young Paul Bryant standing in the third row. Later Bryant would grow up to be the winningest college-football coach of the twentieth century. These were gifts tailored to my enthusiasms.

"Gee guys, I don't know what to say." Handshakes went all round. When the new kid, Uva, shook my hand, he slipped me something, a small disk. Uva was a prematurely balding twenty-four-year-old Kraut, with a stiff new BAMA baseball cap and a metallurgy degree from Hamburg.

"What's this?" I asked.

"I heard you are a Beatles fan."

I nodded.

"It's a bootleg I burned for you, digitally remastered tracks from *Sergeant Pepper*."

He gave me a wink as I slipped it into my pocket.

Here is a secret about the future. One day we will live in our cars. One set of keys for both home and automobile. I know because I design them: cars, buses, the shadowy tractor-trailers that hover for a mile or two in and out of the blind spot of your rear view mirror and inexplicably disappear forever. I design them to run not only on electricity and polonium, but on whims, dreams, states of mind. I pay special attention to spatial relations, ergonomics, the marriage of mood and structure. Five days a week, nine to five, I alone descend into the depths of the inner sanctum of the CAD labs like an ancient and learned abbot, down into the catacombs of the factory where there is hidden an otherwise secret and forbidden library. There I sift through much forgotten

lore and arcana in hopes of recovering something useful or important to the collective spiritual imagination of my people—Alabam-
ians, Southerners, Americans, in that order or reverse—good con-
sumers, one and all. Within the confines of the Vance factory, I am
the engineer with the highest level of for-your-eyes-only security
clearance—clearance to knowledge that can open your mind, your
heart, your pocketbook. I make cars, and my cars make you feel
like you're driving a cathedral.

Picture this. A Super 8 film, *The Bear Bryant Funeral Train*,
begins on a cold day in my hometown, Tuscaloosa, Alabama, near
the banks of the Black Warrior River. It is cold even for January,
an unnatural, mechanical cold. There is a thin rime of black ice
on the roads, and the air carries with it the bitter freon chill of an
old refrigerator running itself into a state of absolute despair. As
the mute rhetoric of the Super 8 reveals, the funeral train is more
than ten miles long and at its maximum width spans the latitude
of eight lumbering Pace Arrow recreation vehicles.

The Bear Bryant Funeral Train is not a real document. It is
a computer-generated film made to look like a document. I have
given the film the grainy look and feel of celluloid to make its content more plausible. Even though my movie is based on a true
story, the truth is not enough. The Super 8 qualities make it more
true—more real. Without the convention of the Super 8, you may
not be able to believe that this many people came to one funeral,
but they did.

As the film begins, the camera's eye travels along a sixty-mile
stretch of road lined with crowds of mourners. They stand in the
misting rain, shoulder to breast, three and four deep, waiting for
a glimpse of the hearse that carries the most important man of
their generation. For those of you too young to remember the

Bear Bryant funeral, the setting is the year nineteen hundred and eighty-three, in the old petrol age—anno Domini, as we used to say in school.

The trouble all started a couple of months ago when my boss, Hans, called me into his office. By then, most of the work on the Bear Bryant Funeral Train Project was done.

"Sorry, Sonny," said Hans. "But it's time for the old dead to make room for the new dead."

I have spent most of my life working as an engineer for Daimler-Chrysler in the Vance factory on the edge of Tuscaloosa. When I first began working here fresh out of college, we made SUVs, the M-class, and later on the more ecofriendly hydrogen-cell M-80 and M-81 models. I've made a lot of money for the Germans over the years. But when Hans told me it was time for me to fade, I didn't kick. I had a multimillion-dollar 401K filled with company stock, and it was clear Hans had troubles.

"Hans . . . you don't think it was me, do you?" There had been some recent problems with corporate theft. Designs for the new solar tractors had turned up missing. And on top of that, someone was tampering with top-secret files from the CAD labs. Protocol mandated that heads had to roll. "You know it's those bastards at Disney again," I said.

Hans was a little pink man with pale blue eyes and a white crew cut; his appearance gave the impression he had been bred for the express purpose of a laboratory experiment. "Shhhh." Hans held his fingers to his lips. "The walls have mice."

Hans walked over to the compact stereo system shaped like an early-twentieth-century Victrola. He whispered "Wagner," his activation word, into the bell. Mysterious waves of dance music filled the room from all directions.

"I've always meant to ask you, what do you say if you actually want to listen to Wagner?"

Hans just grinned mischievously. "Louder," he ordered the Victrola. The machine obeyed. Then he put his arm around me and began to whisper in my ear.

Really, the cars are just part of my job. My real passion is for trains. I used to collect them—first electric model replicas like the Dixie Flyer and the Silver Eagle Express, then the digital choo-choos I downloaded into the wallpaper of my workstation. In college, I took a degree in electrical engineering at the University of Alabama, and when I got the job here at the Vance factory I was sent to Germany for six months to be trained in their new inter-disciplinary architecture program. There we learned how to use the CAD graphics systems to sculpt new automotive designs. We used digital trains all the time to rearrange information in artistic ways. One of our first assignments was to take a medieval diagram of the Great Chain of Being, lay it on its side, and rearrange its links. You could let the whole story of creation unfold like a Mardi Gras parade: it was a grand march of ass-shaking seraphim and garden slugs, cabbages and kings, bears and men.

When I was very young, my parents did their parental duty and took me to Orlando to visit Disney World, which for them was kind of like making a pilgrimage to Mecca. In those days, Orlando was the holy city of the middle class.

I was waiting in line for tickets to Space Mountain when it happened. A man just getting off the ride had a heart attack. He wasn't an old man, maybe forty, but I noticed his face was kind of green as he lumbered out of the darkness of the subterranean roller coaster. I thought he was simply going to vomit as he staggered toward one of the overflowing garbage cans. His left arm fluttered up as he leaned on the trash barrel for support. Then all of a sudden, as if he had been gunned down by a sniper, the man lurched forward and fell over, spilling discarded Cokes and funnel cakes everywhere.

When the paramedics arrived, one of them ripped open the man's button-down. The paramedic placed his ear to his chest. He turned to his partner and shouted, "Massive MI! What if he doesn't make it?"

His partner was already rubbing the paddles of the defibrillator together. "You know the rules. That can't happen. Not inside the park." Then they shocked the roller-coaster victim, and his body arched with electricity.

Around them a crowd had gathered.

Snow White and Goofy looked on in horror.

CAD is an acronym for computer-aided design and it is a friend to architects, engineers, and landscapers everywhere. In the seventeenth century, Descartes developed analytic geometry, which holds that any point on a plane can be specified by a pair of numbers, now called coordinates. Points, lines, and arcs could be described by mathematical equations expressed in terms of X and Y. Then, in the middle of the twentieth century, the American military funded the development of several guidance systems for rockets and other such weapons. These guidance systems became the models for early computers built by IBM. In 1959, IBM and GM set out to build a series of computers that could help them design cars, and in 1961, engineers working on this collaborative project discovered how to create crosshairs on the monitor.

Later that day I stormed into Hans's office. This time he kept the music off.

"You can't just run me out like this."

"It's not just you, Sonny. We are changing all the personnel in the CAD labs. It's become too dangerous for you there. You're better off puttering around on a golf course."

"I'm agoraphobic."

"Don't make this hard on me."

Since the end of the Second World War, the brass at Disney had held a grudge against the Germans. The Nazi propaganda machine had attacked Walt and company as products of a sick American society that glorified vermin, and Disney responded by funneling millions of entertainment dollars into the American war machine and providing American GIs with Mickey Mouse wristwatches with which to synchronize their missions.

Daimler-Benz merged with Chrysler years ago, and now that Mercedes was as American as apple pie, these grudges were no longer supposed to exist. But there were old men in smoke-filled rooms in Pomerania and Uruguay, kept alive with gene therapy and artificial hearts, whose memories stretched deep into the past. A few years ago when Chrysler-Benz bought out Anheuser-Busch, owner of Busch Gardens and Six Flags, we were making it clear to Disney that we were ready to compete with them on their own turf. Many people like me, adept at designing mood-altering rides, were set to work building theoretical roller coasters, concepts for theme-park attractions.

"Be honest, Hans—the mice are gunning for something in the architecture office?"

"Are you still working on your Funeral Train project?"

I nodded. Then I remembered to say, "Yes." Somewhere out there, those large ears were listening. Hans had a plan. A draw play.

"Kill it."

For sure, the Bear Bryant funeral train surpassed the jangling military cavalcade that escorted Jeff Davis into the netherworld. The Davis train started on the steps of the New Orleans City Hall and ended at his sarcophagus, which lay within the gates of the Metarie Cemetery. That was a mere four-mile procession. Many in the parade carried floral arrangements woven into images of cannons, Confederate battle flags, and sabers. But it was hot that summer. No matter how pretty the flowers, their sweet perfume could not hide the stench of Davis's putrefaction.

The Bryant era was a time less of pomp and circumstance and more of heroic joy. No longer did we live within the dispensation of the lost cause. When we put the old man Bryant into the ground, we did it in the epic spirit of Vikings.

The last track on the disk Uva had given me turned out to be a simple video reel, a film of the Bear Bryant funeral procession. I had probably seen this material hundreds of times: on the news, spliced into heart-warming and motivational movies, run on a continuous loop at the University of Alabama's Dionysian homecoming pep rallies, where one watched the footage on a huge screen placed between the Denny Chimes clock tower and a raging bonfire. These pep rallies had all the mystery and magic of a midnight book burning, the air charged with the smell of sweat, sex, and smoke as we burned the visiting team's mascot in effigy and watched the funeral procession of our greatest coach on the big screen. The kid knew that this stock footage was the template for my Funeral Train; now he wanted me to give him the disk with the finished story.

"What are you going to do when you retire?" Uva asked me in his dead, flat, perfect English.

Often in daydreams I have pondered what I would have done with my life if I hadn't spent all my time in the lab testing the structural integrity of the latest DC hydrogen cells and solar tractors on my network station. "With my first pension check, I am going to put a down payment on a vintage Airstream trailer with a 300-horsepower gas combustion engine and 1.7-gallon flush toilet and follow the Crimson Tide to all the great cities of the SEC. I will visit the General Neyland dogwood orchards of Knoxville, the celestial Huey P. Long Stadium in Baton Rouge. I want to go to Georgia and see the newly erected obelisk of Bobby Dodd. Old-fart kind of stuff."

"You know, you have other options."

That's when the kid laid it on me. The offer included wealth, nubile women, and asylum within the walls of the Magic Kingdom. He even hinted that immortality was not out of the question.

The crosshairs changed everything. All of a sudden it was possible to make countless modifications on a single design, whether it be on a car, house, assembly line, or a rose garden. One could build a virtual bridge on the computer and know exactly how much weight it could support, exactly how much wind resistance it could withstand, and so on.

Now we can design a car and never build an expensive prototype—just press a button and send it directly into mass production. On the other hand, it's now also cost-effective to make customized cars specifically tailored for your personality, your lifestyle, your idiosyncrasies. I can design that special car for making a stylish exit from your high-school graduation, or that perfect, pearly white land cruiser to get you from the wedding chapel to Niagara Falls. I can even design a car for when you leave this life. Think of it—a special hearse, just for you.

"My father cried," I told Uva. "When I was invited to be part of the Bryant funeral, he was so proud." Up until that time, my father had never had much use for me. I was a fastidious little blue-eyed snot with precious blond curls. At the age of nine, all I wanted to do was play with my choo-choos. But it was my presence the governor requested in the funeral, and I was henceforth transformed in my father's estimation. "The state needed children to act as mutes, like in a Dickens novel," I told Uva. I was given a little black suit. It had black crushed-velvet lapels and a top hat with a long black bow fixed to the band in the back. "The sleeves were too long, but I loved it. A funeral makes you feel so dignified, especially when you're a kid."

When Uva comes for the exchange, I lead him into the labyrinth of the inner sanctum of the CAD labs, one dark corridor stretches into the next in a spider's web of increasingly narrow hallways—off limits to all but a select few. Finally we reach my private office, a little nook in the heart of the factory no bigger than the janitor's closet, only the walls are decorated with vintage sports paraphernalia—several pennants reading "BAMA vs. Sewanee" and dozens of handbills with rosy Norman Rockwell-esque boys and girls eating Golden Flake potato chips and drinking Coca-Cola as they enjoy the game.

Uva looks around the room, eyes wet with wonder and ambition.

"Watch," I tell him. I load my version of the funeral train into my workstation. Just after the stock footage, there is a cut in the film. The film reopens. The lens focuses on a mighty team of mules, each standing twenty hands high. They have been brought in from a farm in Chattanooga to pull a green cotton wagon behind the hooded Appalachian sin eaters. From the look of them, these mules are monsters, ears flat, milky black-blue eyes, vapor pouring from their near-perfectly round nostrils. The green cotton wagon contains several old women. Even though it's freezing, they wave "Lo, I Knock at the Door" church fans in front of their faces.

It is the lack of sound that captures it all so perfectly. The withered lips mouthing the fa, so, la notes to "Amazing Grace."

"Who are these women?" asks Uva.

"The wagon full of old women represents Bryant's childhood among the hardworking and religious," I say. "It is a known fact that Bryant's mother never attended any of his games because they were too worldly, not even when he played high-school ball in Arkansas."

"The train works on an allegorical level?"

"Allegorical, anagogical, literal. Like an epic poem, they all collapse into one point at the end."

"Ah, you would call this closure."

"Something like that."

It is the lack of music that makes these women beautiful. It is the same power exerted over us by ancient ruins or Roman statues with missing heads. I wish Uva were somewhere else and I were alone in the cloister of the labs. Silence. Sometimes I wish I could write a poem of nothing else.

For over a year now, the Funeral Train has played in a continuous loop on my CAD station. Downloaded and refined in the circuits, in some otherworldly distillation process, the train is in constant flux, always revising itself. I have loaded all the images from the Beatles' *Sergeant Pepper's Lonely Hearts Club Band* album cover and added them into the matrix from which the mourners are randomly selected.

"Until I moved here, I had never heard of this Bryant. Why is he so important? Why choose him as the vehicle for your mood coaster?" Uva wants to know what he is buying.

"Coach Bryant's was the largest funeral procession the post-bellum South had ever seen."

"Bigger than Martin Luther King's?"

"Oh yes."

"Than Elvis's?"

"Without a doubt." What Uva failed to understand was this: Coach Bryant lived in the premerger era. He was a demagogue, and he carried a cult-of-personality aura similar to that of Hitler and Gandhi. He was our patriarch, and we revered him as a sort of superlative invention of the South. He was our Nietzsche in houndstooth, wielding his gridiron will-to-power like an ax handle. A walking-tall, redneck ubermensch. "When he was alive, his very presence inspired . . . terror and joy."

"As does the film."

"Maybe. I think of the film as more like Greek tragedy. A poetic re-creation of the mythic past."

"Pity and fear, then?"

"Maybe. Maybe just fear."

In the old days, no one in Tuscaloosa drove a Mercedes except for maybe a few divorce lawyers. Those were dark times, before the sport utility vehicle. Tuscaloosa had no smiling, bilingual executives like Hans or Uva, no need for Montessori day care or Starbucks.

"In this town," I say, "up until the death of the Bear, all we needed was football to be happy." I feel myself getting a little misty with nostalgia. "Oh how we had loved to watch our beautiful sons smash into one another, crushing knuckles and breaking ribs." We were fascinated with the elusive quality of youth. I cry out, suddenly, "And the cheerleaders, what angels."

In my mind I summon up a picture of a blonde in a crimson skirt, a crimson *A* on her breast, her arms raised in victorious salute, armpits shaved smooth as panes of glass, and then I picture what she might look like if inserted into the Train.

Uva looks startled. "We wouldn't use the Train to hurt anyone, you know. We want to use it to help us build a new coaster. That's what you want, isn't it? You don't want Hans to kill it, do you?"

I think about the man dying in the mouth of Space Mountain, the unholy crowd gawking around him, doing nothing, waiting for the paramedics to shock him back to life.

After the retirement party's Cokes and cake, I had gone back to my cubicle, where I proceeded to test the wind resistance on one of our electromagnetically refrigerated transport trucks. Only I could hear Doogie Sims talking to Uva, in whispers. I could tell there was a general sense of agreement in their murmurs. Was Doogie in on it? A double agent?

"Did you ask him if it were true, about the Funeral Train?" Doogie asked.

"What?"

"You know he was there. When he was a kid."

"At the funeral?"

"*In* the funeral," said Doogie.

"A participant?"

The film resumes on the steps of the First Methodist Church of Tuscaloosa, with a group of stalwart-looking pallbearers, former linemen, loading the mahogany coffin into a mammoth hearse with long black fins. There are little black curtains on the doors, and on the side is a window-unit air conditioner. The Bear had loved air-conditioning.

"As I recall, there had been no elaborate funeral oration within the church before we buried him in Birmingham," I tell Uva. No eulogizing. No choir. Only a few tears and a little organ music that wafted from the corners of the packed church. Closed-circuit TV cameras recorded this part of the funeral, as many other mourners paid their respects at nearby churches, watching the service on wide-screen TVs.

"Why bury him in Birmingham?"

"His wife, Mary Harmon—her family was from there." But the real funeral wasn't in Birmingham or in the church; it was outside on the streets. The eulogy was the unfolding parade itself, a living Bayeaux tapestry unfurled down University Boulevard. A wreath was hung on the Cadillac's back door as we began our long, slow journey into the city.

Behind the hearse stands a congregation of Appalachian sin eaters in black cassocks. Like many southern demagogues such as Wallace and Long, the Bear had a taste for strong drink and fast women. It is the job of the sin eaters to consume these paltry sins along with the more formidable transgressions caused by pride. The names of these sins have been written down on little slips of paper and baked in several pans of cornbread, which the sin eaters will feast upon as they commit Bryant's body to the grave. These sin eaters are broad, stout men, well-fed on the weakness of others.

"It was also their job to carry us, all the little mutes, on their shoulders. That's me right there." I point toward the edge of the screen at a little boy, blond hair stuffed under the black top hat.

Uva nods as if he understands what I am talking about. But how could he?

There is a cut in the Super 8, and for a moment the screen goes black.

The Bear Bryant funeral train moved with the quiet dignity displayed at all great obsequies. Martin Luther King's hundred thousand mourners in Atlanta showed no more meek and humble reverence when they lowered their leader into the earth. The Bryant procession was much bigger and grander than even the glitzy, white-Cadillac flotilla that carried Elvis through the chartered streets of Memphis. There were no food vendors or T-shirt salesmen in the Bryant train. Certainly there were no florists along the highway, only the fans, nine hundred thousand of them holding signs that read, "We miss you Coach."

As a reporter from the *Tuscaloosa News* wrote the next day, "The Bear Bryant funeral train was a cheerless tailgate party, with no food or libation to warm the crowd."

As the film resumes, the next car in the train tells how the Bear won his name. A grizzly, on loan from the Birmingham Zoo, sits next to a farm boy in overalls, who holds the bear firmly on a leash.

"Bryant earned his name in 1925 at the Lyric Theater. He

agreed to wrestle a carnival bear for his hometown's entertainment. I think secretly he was trying to impress a girl."

"And he won?"

The grizzly rides its parade float calmly, almost sleepily, next to the serious farm boy.

"When it looked like the boy was going to beat the old, frazzled bear, the owner jerked off its muzzle and it mauled him."

After the boy and bear comes the University of Alabama's Million Dollar Band.

"I think I remember them playing a New Orleans dirge," I say.

"Dirge?"

"A funeral song. Something they must have picked up from one of their trips to the Sugar Bowl."

The drum major is dressed as a voodoo priest, the faces of his band mates painted like skeletons. Then come the parade floats decorated by the fraternities and sororities. Huge crepe-paper elephants roll along the asphalt, each carrying a flag reading "Roll Tide Roll" in its trunk.

Here comes the march of teams, car after car of aged football players, players from Maryland and Kentucky, players from Texas A&M. Finally, the players from the Crimson Tide. Over forty teams in all, most of them wearing red jerseys. Those too fat to fit into their uniforms carry them under their arms. Here comes the march of heroes. Here comes Bart Starr and Big John Hannah. Here comes the "Italian Stallion" Johnny Musso and "Mr. Tackle" Billy Neighbors. Here comes Ken "Snake" Stabler. Here comes Joe "Willie" Namath with his wobbly weak knees and his black aviator shades to hide the tears.

Championship teams carry banners. So many of them pass by that, after a while, it seems as if they are all the same team marching forward down the road, as well as backward through time, getting younger and younger as they progress forward. It looks as if the Super 8 is moving in both fast-forward and reverse; the faces of the athletes glow with a sheen of ruined youth that has long since fallen away. Behind them the majorettes twirl flaming batons. They seem to hover a millimeter or so above the spinning earth. Then come the fans in their vans, RVs, and mobile homes.

Behind the parade of fans comes the motorcade of foreign ambassadors: parliamentarians from the Hague, senators from the Kineset, Politburo members. There is at least one Chinese field marshal. There is a caravan of oil sheiks from Yemen with fine barbered beards and almond eyes. The choleric Soviet prime minister Andropov is there, clearly drunk, and so is the black-bearded writer Solzhenitsyn, down from Vermont. Idi Amin, in a sky-blue Eldorado convertible with leopard-skin interior, waves at the crowd. From the Sergeant Pepper matrix of mourners, only John Lennon and Johnny Weismuller wave back.

The eldest son of Ho Chi Min, Ben Pheu, rides near the end of the train. He has come to America to research Civil War reenactments at Gettysburg and Antietam and has stumbled upon a most impressive ceremony.

I point Ben Pheu out to Uva. "When Ho died, his funeral was just like this."

Then comes the caboose of the train. "Here," I tell Uva, "is the greatest football fan in the world at the time. In his own country he was something of a god, where he was revered and worshipped."

There is a look of fearful recognition on Uva's face. I whisper a song of menace in his ear: "M-I-C . . . K-E-Y . . ."

Several barbarous dwarves in Ray Ban sunglasses run alongside the last convertible, one hand held to the transistor radios in their ears. The car's diplomatic flag flutters in the wind.

There is something majestic about it, even now, especially since I already know what is about to happen. Even Uva knows what is about to happen, though he hopes it will not.

Muddied sunlight reflects off the hood of the car, momentarily blinding the camera.

The massive, dignified head tips to the side, his ears as big as satellite dishes; the unwavering plastic smile is now almost vertical. The official concubine can't stop waving. She is not as solemn as the rest of the funeral train, in her polka dots and pink pillbox hat.

The camera shakes, turns sideways, rights itself.

The crowd scatters. The concubine clutches the string of pearls at her throat.

Did he scream behind the smile when the first bullet pierced his wrist and smashed into his pelvis?

Mothers fall on children.

Husbands on wives.

Aleister Crowley falls on top of the Vargas Girl.

Duck and cover.

The dwarves draw their Walthers, pointing them in all directions. Only there isn't enough time to discern that the shots are coming from the clock tower, from the carillion on the quadrangle, Denny Chimes.

Another shot and the entire train begins to fall like a row of dominos toward the hearse, which by now is halfway to Birmingham.

The driver of the hearse hits his brakes and the Bear's coffin spills out the back door and slides along the slick black ice. The team of demonic mules attempts to run in different directions, toppling the old women out of the green cotton wagon and splitting the yoke apart.

"Halt!" Just at that moment, Hans and his security team burst into the room, making an awful racket in their jackboots.

Uva screams, "No, please . . . I don't know how . . ." But the captain of the guard smashes him in the face with a billy club, and the poor metallurgist falls to the ground like a rag doll. From this point on, things won't go well for Uva.

The third slug from the bolt-action is the head shot. This is the part that becomes more unbelievable each time I watch it. The massive mouse skull splits apart like a plaster cast, leaving exactly one half of the unwavering smile. I stop the film, roll the counter back a few seconds, and then call up the crosshairs on the monitor to lock the XY coordinates on the skull.

"Watch this," I tell Hans. "I added a little 'fuck you' here at the end."

Hans beams. "Fine job, Sonny." He pats me on the back.

I can retire in peace now. I can retire the Train, too, now that it has served its true purpose. I have drawn out the mole, killed the mouse, kept Tuscaloosa safe from the encroaching tendrils of the Magic Kingdom for another day.

I hit *play* as the security guards drag Uva's limp body into the elevator. I am hoping to pinpoint the very instant that everything changes. Everything that came before this moment must be reconfigured in our imagination as leading up to this event. Everything that happens after can only be perceived as a result of this taking place.

We watch as the mouse's skull splits apart again. Even though we both know the Bear Bryant Funeral Train is merely a dream-like hoax, neither Hans nor I can turn away.

The camera jerks back and to the left.

Back and to the left.

The Flannery O'Connor Award for Short Fiction

David Walton, *Evening Out*
Leigh Allison Wilson, *From the Bottom Up*
Sandra Thompson, *Close-Ups*
Susan Neville, *The Invention of Flight*
Mary Hood, *How Far She Went*
François Camoin, *Why Men Are Afraid of Women*
Molly Giles, *Rough Translations*
Daniel Curley, *Living with Snakes*
Peter Meinke, *The Piano Tuner*
Tony Ardizzone, *The Evening News*
Salvatore La Puma, *The Boys of Bensonhurst*
Melissa Pritchard, *Spirit Seizures*
Philip F. Deaver, *Silent Retreats*